HAMPTON ROAD

by Michael Segedy

ISBN-13: 978-1466211278
Copyright © 2004 by Michael Segedy
Third Edition, August 2013

Cover by Travis Miles of probookcovers.com

what if a much of a which of a wind
gives the truth to summer's lie;
bloodies with dizzying leaves the sun
and yanks immortal stars awry?

what if a dawn of a doom of a dream
bites this universe in two,
peels forever out of his grave
and sprinkles nowhere with me and you?

e.e. cummings

CHAPTER ONE

I'm eighteen now. Just turned eighteen last month. At least I think it was last month. Apparently there's no one here I can confide in on that matter. Yesterday I asked Stockton what day it was, and he said it was Friday, July the first. What a damn lie! And I told him so. It couldn't be July the first because last month was my birthday and my birthday is April the third.

"Well, you'll have to ask Phillips about that," he said indifferently, in this husky voice of his that is half a put-on. He was letting on that if he didn't want to discuss the date, then it wouldn't be discussed. He looks like a washed-up linebacker for the New York Jets. He's around six four, neck-less, fat, about as wide as a barn door, and about as smart. His face is big and round and white with these small narrowly set eyes, which give off about as much light as a flashlight with dead batteries. Anyway, I guess he thought his friggin' size would intimidate me so that I'd just clam up.

But I was insistent. "Phillips? For cryin' out loud! Why in hell do I *need* to ask Phillips what day it is?"

"Look, kid, just ask Phillips. Okay?"

"Yeah, sure. Then tell Phillips I want to see him right now!" I shouted. I was sick of his that's-not-my-department replies. That was the biggest problem here. No one ever seemed to have any answers, including Phillips.

1

"Look, you know you'll see Phillips during your session later today. Right now I would like you just to take your medicine," he said, noticeably piqued. In the palm of a large doughy hand, he held out two small brown capsules. His hand was as white as his pants and the two brown tablets looked obscene, like two bird droppings. Worse yet, he was asking me to swallow the disgusting things. The six-foot-four Pillsbury doughboy was asking me to swallow bird droppings! And every day I had to go through the same routine. The big white blob and his tiny bird-shit pills. Well, not today. Today would be different.

"I don't think I need to take any pills," I said. "Anyway, they look like bird shit."

"They're your medicine," he replied sharply. "The same medicine you take every morning before breakfast."

"What day is it?" I asked again, this time with palpable defiance. I watched his face change from a pale white to a bright crimson, like I'd slapped him or something. A fiery red started at the base of his stumpy neck and spread like a brush fire over his face. His beady little hawk eyes narrowed and grew even darker as they locked on me like he was lookin' through a gun sight.

"Are you going to take your medicine?" He turned and glanced quickly toward the door. "Or do you want me to cram this bird-shit, as you call it, into your foul little beak?"

I swung my right leg and then my left over the chrome bed rail. My feet didn't reach the floor, and the thought made me feel odd. I stared into his ruddy face and imagined for a moment that I saw steam escaping from its pores. Then I tried to muster up a bit of courage. I thought of Charlie and how he always looked up to me. "Hot Shoe Billy," he would say, grinning. I was sort of his hero, I guess. Now I had to show this jerk that I wasn't going to let him just push me around.

"'What day is it?' isn't a real tough question now, is it?" I said, cracking my knuckles. "Surely your knowledge goes beyond counting out pills and cleaning bedpans. What do you say we play a little game? A calendar game. If you don't know the names of all the months then I…"

He reached into his pocket and pulled out his beeper.

"Pete, I'm having a little problem here in 214."

The next thing I knew the great white whale and three of his cronies had me pinned to the bed. One of them tried to stuff the pills in my mouth, but I clamped down on his finger and drew blood.

"Shit!" he screamed, and then I felt a fist come down like a boulder. It was a real sleazy, cheap shot. A sharp pain shot up through my stomach and knotted in my throat. I instinctively opened my mouth to draw in air, and before I could yell out, he thrust the two pills in and forced my jaws closed until I swallowed.

That was yesterday.

Later, the same afternoon, I told Phillips about all of this, and he said he would "look into it."

"Sure," I said, "and while you're at it, maybe you can tell me why I have to take this friggin' medicine every day."

"It will help you remember things," he said.

"What things? What is it that you want me to remember? You see, I'm a little confused about what's going on here. And who you are exactly. And I don't think the medicine is making things any easier. What day is it anyway?" I said out of exasperation.

"It's July the first, three days before Independence Day."

So today's July the second, two days before the Indy Mile, and I'm supposed to be there. Charlie and I have made plans to go down together in the shop van with Chuck, my mechanic and tuner. The track's only a six hours drive away. I wanted Praxy to come along, but her parents would never agree to that. Especially her father. He's this tall, goofy dentist who thinks he's something special. He lets me know in no uncertain terms that Praxy's family and my family are from the opposite side of the tracks.

The opposite side of the tracks. That's an expression my old man used all the time. He'd say that life was tough for those born on the wrong side of the tracks. I guess his drinking was a way of forgetting about the tracks. I remember him sitting around in his sleeveless T-shirt, on the sofa in the living room. He would sit there with his bottle of Wild Irish Rose, like it was some magic lamp, squeezing it between his knees and rubbing it like he was expecting a genie to pop out and grant him three wishes. I often wonder what his wishes would have been if a genie would have appeared.

Yeah, so unlike Praxy's old man. He's as stiff and antiseptic as the bristles on a new toothbrush. Makes you want to puke every time you see him parading about in his sporty hundred-dollar blazers. He's the kind of guy who wears a suit and tie to a high school basketball game. What a loser! I remember going with Charlie once to this basketball game and watching Praxy walk in with her father in his Brooks Brothers suit. When she saw me, I thought she was going to have a meltdown. Everybody else in the place was dressed normally. I had on my scruffy leather jacket, the one I bought at a swap meet about a year ago. It's one of those retro jackets with a black wool collar and wool cuffs. Looks like a World War II aviation jacket. I joke with Charlie all the time because right after I bought mine, he went out and purchased one of these fake jackets that kind of looks similar. Cost him about three hundred bucks. It even comes with imitation scuffmarks! Can you believe that? It's supposed to make it look real authentic, like maybe it was a paratrooper's who was shot down in it. It's funny all the planning and research that goes into producing fake things, like phony scuffmarks. I remember kidding him and telling him that I'd trade him…

That's odd. Real friggin' odd. Suddenly I can feel my heart racing like I just swallowed a handful of Dexedrine tablets. Maybe it's a side effect of the medicine. What a strange sensation. And all at once.

One minute I'm fine and the next it's like someone snapped a photo inches from my face with a high power flash, and then this light-headedness. Gee, I feel like I could float right out the goddamn window. God, I feel giddy. It has to be the pills. I'll have to write all of this down. That's what the notebook here on the nightstand is for. I'll have to mention it to Phillips at our session later on today.

CHAPTER TWO

"Dad, you sure you want to go to the game? There's a Tom Cruise movie playing at the mall," Praxy teased. She knew he was a sucker for Tom Cruise movies. She wanted to see if he'd take the bait.

"Are you kidding?" he laughed. "This is a title game. I wouldn't miss it for anything. Show some loyalty to your alma mater. You guys walloped Franklin last weekend. And tonight you're playing for the regional title. If you win this game, you'll be in it for the state title."

Mr. Bishop missing a home game was about as likely as the president of General Motors missing a board meeting. Praxy wasn't all that thrilled about going to her school's basketball games, especially home games, but she'd go to please her father. He had never missed a home game as far as she could remember. He had played college basketball for a small private Midwestern school, and anytime there was a home game, he would try to coax Praxy into going with him. She liked sports all right. It was jocks she couldn't stand. In her mind, though, basketball players were kind of excluded from their ranks. She couldn't imagine her father as a jock. Every time she thought of him in basketball shorts and a jersey, she had to suppress laughing out loud. Her father, the athlete! And look at him now. He still had the tall, slender frame of a basketball player, and the shoe size, (that's where she got her size nines), but the rest of him was all dentist. He looked like a dentist, smelled like a dentist, and even had this annoying habit of fixing his eyes on your teeth when he talked to you and giving them a quick going-over. It was rather unnerving. Praxy mustered up the courage once to confront him about it. While he was going over one of her lab reports with her, he kept looking up at her teeth.

"Dad, is there something wrong with my teeth?"

"No, Prax. Why?"

"Well, I have this feeling that you're checking them out for braces or something."

"Really?" he said, truly surprised. "You have perfectly straight teeth."

She'd decided many times to give up pointing out any of her father's foibles. If she really wanted to pick on something, it would be his overly formal way of dressing for basketball games. Dinner was almost over, and they would have to leave in about thirty minutes. Most fathers would change into slacks and a sweatshirt, or jeans and a flannel shirt, or something down-to-earth. The problem was he didn't have anything casual to change into, at least nothing that was a part of his winter wardrobe.

No, that wasn't exactly correct. He did have a new button-down flannel shirt and a pair of Levi's jeans she had given him for his birthday the winter before, though she hadn't seen him wear them but once or twice. And that was when he was doing yard work. Most of the year, except for a two-week vacation during the summer, he would be decked out in a blazer and dress pants.

No one went to the games dressed like he did. Wearing a checkered tweed blazer and shiny silk tie. The tie looked like an artifact from the pre-sixties. So did her father for that matter. His glasses were heavy black-rimmed bifocals that made him look like some nerdy accountant. She would be the only student whose father came to basketball games dressed for the theater.

As she thought about her father, she felt a tinge of guilt. Why should she be embarrassed about the way he dressed? Did he tell her what to wear? Well, yes, in a way. Not always with words, but with these painful grimaces that gave one the impression that he was suffering a gas attack. Maybe had too much cabbage for dinner. He tried not to be the lecturing type, though he rarely succeeded in keeping out of the pulpit, especially the couple of times when Billy's name popped up. That was the funny thing. She was afraid to point out to her own father that wearing formal attire to a basketball game just wasn't "cool." Why? Because she respected his individuality. Then why couldn't he respect Billy's? Probably because he had a warped image of guys and motorcycles. He grew up with the idea that anyone who rode a motorcycle was a Hell's Angel or some Marlon Brando type, like in the old classic *The Wild One*. Some duck-tailed vandal who wanted to take over the town and then run off with the soda jerk's daughter.

Many people had a problem with individuality, not just her father. For most it was a great idea, that is, as long as it didn't offend the majority's sensibilities. Now anyone who was really different--say the pin-through-the-cheek type or the girl with the spiky green hair--wasn't expressing individualism. She was just plain crazy. And threatening. And yet America was founded on the rights of the individual. The right to be different. At least that's what they had taught her in school. There was this guy she had read about in her American literature class who had said, "Whoso would be a man must be a nonconformist!" She couldn't remember his name, but that wasn't important. It was the idea behind it that mattered.

Praxy watched a small cloud of steam rise from the serving spoon as her father scooped green beans with white sauce onto his plate. His hands were as soft and silky as the shirt he had on. From all the time spent in the office, she thought.

"Honey, would you like me to pass you some more mashed potatoes?" her mother asked, noticing his plate was half empty.

"Yes, please. And some more gravy, too."

Praxy lifted the napkin from her lap and set it down lightly on the dining room table. She looked up from her plate and then shot a tentative glance over at her mother. Her eyes settled on her mother for a few uncomfortable seconds as she squirmed around a bit in her chair, pushing two curly, blond tendrils from in front of her large brown eyes.

"Dad, you think you're gonna have time to change before we leave for the game?" she said with forced nonchalance.

"Yes, honey, why don't you change into something more comfortable?" her mother coaxed.

Good ole mom. Such a diplomat. She had dedicated a large part of her life, it seemed, to striking compromises and engineering reconciliations. Her once shiny black hair was now without luster and streaked with gray. And her countenance, tired and matronly, belonged to an older person, not to a woman just turning forty. The once soft, delicate lines that had traced the contours of her face had hardened some.

"Maybe you could put on those snazzy jeans Prax bought you for your birthday last winter. Also, don't forget that the gym has concrete bleachers and they're always dirty and when you sit down on them…" she hurried the words out, attempting some humor, "you're gonna have some dusty britches."

No doubt she was beautiful once, and in those days her father must have been madly in love with her. Sometimes when they were alone and her mother was in one of her rare philosophical moods, she would become winsome and her talk would turn to an old beau she had before she met and fell insanely in love with Bobby Bishop. Listening to her, Praxy could imagine a time when love must have been like a whirlwind spinning her heart around and around like some crazy top.

"Might get my bottom dusted?" her father said, breaking her reverie. "Won't be the first time. Let's just hope the same doesn't happen to our Cavaliers," he chuckled.

And now? Well, there were still the flowers her father never failed to have delivered to her mother on special occasions, like her birthday, Valentine's Day, or their anniversary. And, of course, there were still their special nights out together, once or twice a month. This generally meant having dinner at some fancy restaurant and then taking in a movie, or maybe even going to the theater. Her mother tried never to miss any of the popular performances at the Weathervane, a small local theater outside of town. Before going to bed in the evenings, they would sometimes sit on the sofa holding hands and watching the late news. Yet their love seemed so sedate, so tame, so adult. Praxy wondered if this was the way of love. Was the magic one discovers in romance only a spring or summer thing? When winter's gray clouds stretch across the horizon, do the swallows that flutter wildly in lovers' hearts fly the coop? Or just settle down for a long, cozy rest? In her parents' case, it seemed to be the latter. More often than not, Praxy imagined them as two comic old lovebirds, a genteel rooster and a matronly hen, nesting down for the duration.

"Whoso would be a man must be a nonconformist," she said wistfully.

"What was that, honey?" her father asked.

"Whoso would be a man must be a nonconformist."

"Why, that's Emerson, isn't it?" Her mother's face glowed. "It's been years since I've read Emerson."

"Yeah, Mom. We were studying him in English class. He was pretty weird, believed in something called transcendentalism. I'm still not certain what that means exactly. It has something to do with the idea that man and God are part of the same spirit. Mrs. Graystone told us it was a lot like Hinduism. I guess what impressed me though was what Emerson had to say about the individual and about nonconformity."

She could read a kind of puzzled look on her father's face, which made sense since she rarely waxed literary at the dinner table.

"Billy wrote this essay on nonconformity, and Mrs. Graystone read it to the class." There, she'd said it. Billy's name again. And she could feel her cheeks burning like hot coals, but she didn't care. The cards were dealt, and now it was her father's turn to call or fold.

"Billy? Oh, yeah, Billy Salino…"

"Billy Solinski, Dad," she said.

"Yes, the kid with the motorcycles. He races them, doesn't he?"

"That's right, Dad, and he turned professional last year. Anyway, he wrote this essay on nonconformity, and when Mrs. Graystone read it to the class, the class was so quiet you could have heard an eyelash flutter. It was so…so much like Billy. I mean, if anyone is a nonconformist, he is."

"Turned professional?"

"Yes, he has a pro license," Praxy said, her heart racing to keep up with her thoughts. "And in just one year he has advanced to the Junior professional level. Actually, he has done better than that. He is in first place in the state's rankings, in his classification that is, and plans to turn Expert this year."

"Expert is the top ranking?" her father mused.

"Yes. You start out as a Pro-Am, and then, if you get the points, you become a Junior, like Billy is now. And after that an Expert. When he becomes an Expert

13

early next year, he's talking about competing on the national circuit. He already has two motorcycle shops and some local businesses sponsoring him."

"Seems like you have learned a whole lot about motorcycle racing these last few months," her mother laughed.

"And with all this racing business going on, what will he do about school? He's in the same grade as you. Isn't that right?" The conversation had suddenly taken another turn.

"Yeah, he's a junior."

"Only a junior? How old is he?"

"I think I'll have some coffee," Praxy's mother quickly interjected. "Let me take your plates out to the kitchen. Dear, would you like some coffee?"

Good ole mom. Always trying to smooth things over. This was just another one of her attempts to make the conversation as light as Angel Food cake. And her father, it was just like him. So vigilant. Watching out for his daughter so she wouldn't get in with the wrong bunch. Arranging her future for her. And Billy and motorcycles clearly didn't fit in with *his* vision of her future happiness. Too often he came across like he was the only one who could possibly know anything about her happiness. And taking his daughter to the regional basketball playoffs was right at the top! It was this unsolicited meddling in her private affairs--she was nearly old enough to vote--that was beginning to get under her skin. But would she ever show it? No, not his sweet, loving daughter. Inside she could be seething, but outside, calm, complaisant Praxy. God! She played the part of the compliant daughter with Academy Award-winning poise. How many times had she denied expressing her true feelings to him? Yes, she was her mother's daughter all right. That became more and more apparent each day, and less tolerable.

"I don't think we'll have time for coffee," he said, glancing at his watch. As Praxy watched him get up from the table, she could see he didn't feel that it was important to pursue the topic of Billy any further. No, in his own mind, he had made his point quite effectively--had thrown the dart and managed to hit the bull's-eye. A painless, but effective hit. Painless for him.

Praxy looked down at her plate and swallowed hard. Her throat was dry, and she felt hot all over inside. She listened to the running water in the kitchen sink and her mother scraping the scraps of food from the plates into the disposal. The sounds seemed distant. Her own silence had stirred something in her. Standing across the table from her, her father seemed taller than usual. For an instant, she imagined him as some shadowy character from the Old Testament, an Abraham or Joshua, a stony biblical figure standing over her in judgment. And over Billy.

And what did he know about Billy? He raced motorcycles and to her father that was enough. No young man who thought seriously about his future would race motorcycles. They were dangerous, and by association so was Billy. How little her father really knew.

She had had two boyfriends before Billy. Of the three, Billy, leather-jacketed and all, would receive the Gentleman Award if she were the one to pass it out.

Before dating Billy, there was Tony Andronotti, jerk extraordinaire, though it took her a longer time than it should have to figure that out. With him, their dates always began and ended the same way. They would drive up to Blandon Cliff and sit in his convertible listening to the radio. And then he would put his plan into effect, seeing how many buttons he could undo before the song ended. He was slicker than Houdini. The only difference was that his magic tricks involved trying to get her to become the escape artist by slipping out of something. She thought she liked him, at first anyway. He was really cute, a blue-eyed Italian with curly black hair. He was also a star on the football team, so most of the girls at school were crazy about him. Maybe that's what attracted her. That and his Italian charisma. Well, anyway, it wore off after it was clear what he really wanted and clear what she didn't want. Also, she began to feel like she was just going out with him because he was popular. It made her a hypocrite to her real feelings about him. It was like dating some teenage Hugh Jackman. A little too macho for her tastes. The whole thing was crazy, so she just stopped seeing him, which didn't seem to break his big Italian heart much.

God, Billy was sure different. He wasn't the kind of guy whose fingers were all over you the second you were alone with him. Nor was he some egomaniac trying to impress you all the time, like Tony had. That was another thing about Tony. Whenever they'd leave school together, he would have to squeal his car tires. He wanted everyone to see his red BMW convertible. It was part of his macho act. The car was a gift from his father, a birthday present. His father actually presented it to him in a huge gift box wrapped in sparkly silver paper with a gigantic red ribbon. How tacky. His father was filthy rich. He made his money in the restaurant business--owned a dozen or more fast-food restaurants all over town. He was this old, fat, balding Italian who looked like Vitto Corleone in *The Godfather*.

No, Billy didn't have a fancy red convertible to cruise around town in, nor a rich father. He didn't have a father at all. He lived alone with his mother. She thought again about her father's remark. "Only a junior? How old is he?" It was true he had been retained a year, and it was also true that her father would try to make a big deal out of that. But her father didn't know the whole story either, how Billy had missed all of second grade. Billy told her once that his father used to change jobs more often than the average guy changes oil in his car. As a result, Billy had attended more than ten different schools.

No, Billy wouldn't squeal his tires in front of the school if he had a fancy sports car. What made Billy so special and so attractive was that he never tried to impress anyone. He said what he thought, and his thoughts were spoken from his heart, because Billy knew where he stood. He knew who he was. More than anyone she had ever known.

"Well, Prax, you ready?" her father asked, stepping away from the table. His words jolted her back to the present.

"Sure, Dad, whenever you're ready."

She had managed to evade any confrontation and to conceal her fears, as well as forgo any hope for mutual understanding. *Whoso would be a man must be a nonconformist.* Was it really that difficult to face him? She couldn't help but associate her lack of resolve with her inability to discover in herself the simple honesty that she had discovered in Billy. That was the source of real courage. Knowing yourself and acting accordingly. You had to look inside, not outside. If you couldn't find anything at the source, what was the point in looking for it elsewhere?

CHAPTER THREE

Before Charlie and Billy started hanging around together, Charlie had attended all the school's basketball games. He loved basketball. In junior high, he had played point guard for the Wakefield Junior High Eagles, and he was quite good. In fact, he was the points leader for the season. Then he went out for the high school team in his freshman year, but at five-nine, he ended up having his shots blocked or the ball batted out of his hands whenever he went for a layup. He soon realized that short stature was about as valuable to a basketball player as a speech impediment is to a sports commentator. Before long, it became clear to him that his major contribution to the team would be warming the bench.

"Why don't we grab that place down below?" Charlie said, pointing to a spot near center court in the middle of the fourth row, large enough for two or three people to squeeze in.

"Yeah, okay. From the looks of things, you'd think there was gonna be a Michael Jackson concert here tonight," Billy said good-humoredly.

The tumult grew as more people poured into the gym's large windowless structure. Charlie could barely make out Billy's comment about Michael Jackson, though he was right next to him. A young couple forced their way past Charlie and Billy. The woman was holding a screaming baby. Two rows down from where they stood, three kids were playfully shoving each other about when one of them pitched forward into a burly guy in a flannel shirt. The place was packed. In a few minutes there wouldn't be any standing room. During the pep rally at school, Mr. Madison, the principal, mentioned that the mayor himself was planning to attend.

Charlie and Billy worked their way down the rows of bleachers to the place they had spotted from above. As he sat down on the hard concrete steps, Charlie felt the cold dampness of the concrete against his tailbone. He looked around and noticed that many people had brought cushions. He felt stupid for not strapping a couple of the cushions onto the back of his Honda. He'd forgotten how cold bleachers could get in the winter months.

He had just thought about mentioning his oversight to Billy when both teams came onto the court. They started warming up by queuing up and practicing layups. McKinley had on shiny blue jerseys and blue shorts with yellow stripes. Oak Creek's red and black uniforms looked tawdry by comparison. Charlie wondered if the school had purchased the new uniforms especially for this game to boost morale and school spirit. Or maybe that was just part of it. Since the mayor would be attending the game, Mr. Madison would want his boys to look their best. What a brownnoser, Charlie thought. There was not an ounce of sincerity in the guy. Madison and his tight-faced smirk. He was about as warm and understanding as a weasel's smile. Someday he would probably be superintendent of schools. No doubt about it. He had all the disingenuousness of a prize politician.

Since hanging around Billy, Charlie's thoughts had become more political. Charlie's own opinion of politics and politicians paled next to Billy's. He once told Charlie that the student council was nothing more or less than a breeding grounds for future dissemblers. And that someday, with practice, and with role models like Madison, they'd grow into polished hypocrites. Billy's expression for them was shameless sham artists. And John Gilmore was a perfect example. John Gilmore was the president of the student council. Once he gave a speech in front of the entire school on "The Evils of Marijuana," followed by a month-long campaign against the "evil weed." He and his cronies created shameless propaganda posters to display all over school. One poster even had a magazine cut-out of a deformed baby with this pregnant, sixties-type hippie mother in the background smoking a joint. Such a brilliant propaganda collage! Then each day he would put an anti-drug piece, a quote that he lifted out of the *National Review,* in the school bulletin. Billy called him Johnny Goebels Gilmore, after the infamous Nazi propagandist and Hitler's right-hand man. Gilmore said the aim of the campaign was to help create at school "an awareness of the dangers of drug abuse." Such a glaring hypocrite. At more than one party, Charlie had seen him and his friends all red-eyed and reeking of pot. John Gilmore was a perfect example of Billy's idea of the phony politician. Billy told Charlie that Gilmore probably would be elected to the United States Senate someday, or maybe even become president, and then he too could admit that he'd once smoked pot, but never inhaled.

Billy had gotten yanked out of his U.S. Government class once because of his outspoken views on politics. Well, that was part of it. He also loathed Coach Wilkins, and Wilkins knew it. The class was discussing the national elections, and Wilkins asked Billy his opinion on the presidential debates. Billy had said that he really didn't think Coach Wilkins would want to hear it, but the coach had insisted. So he'd told him. He said politics as he saw it was the science and practice of deceit, its main function being to discover what Mr. Average American wants and convincing him that you would give it to him. And he'd get it all right! Billy concluded his comment by saying that Aristotle once said that any man running for a political office isn't worthy of it. "Good ole Aristotle," Billy said with this ear-to-ear grin. "Maybe we should spend more time studying Greek philosophy and less time trying to figure out if we're Democrats or Republicans. The shit's a waste of time."

Coach Wilkins's face had turned three shades redder than the stripes on Old Glory. He had ordered Billy to step out in the hall, and then he had stormed out behind him. After a minute or more of listening to Wilkins's screaming tirade, Billy had reentered the room, taken his seat, and stared out the window in disbelief. Wilkins had tried to resume class discussion on the elections, but the ole wind had been knocked out of his sail, as they say, and the bell had sounded a few minutes later.

Many of the latecomers who could not find seats were now standing against the sidewalls of the gym or sitting in the aisles. Charlie couldn't help but notice this huge flabby man seated four or five rows down and

22

slightly to the front and left of them. He was more than a yard wide and dressed in a blue-striped polo shirt that stretched like a sausage skin over his obese frame. The thick rolls of fat spilling over his girth were held in suspension by the thin, elastic fabric of his polo shirt. The shirt acted like a dam, and Charlie wondered what would happen if one of the elastic seams in the dam split. The man fumbled with his pocket and then finally extracted something small, like hard candies. Charlie watched his small chubby hand go repeatedly to his mouth, like some gambling addict feeding a slot machine. Directly behind him sat a small girl, perhaps six or seven years old, sandwiched in-between her mother and father. She kept trying to look around the wall of flesh. The girl's parents completely ignored her efforts to see beyond the huge man. They yakked back and forth, the father gesticulating spasmodically at the players, while the little girl remained in a kind of crossfire.

"Think I should say something?" Charlie asked, pointing at the couple, the little girl, and the obese man.

"What did you have in mind?"

"I don't know. Maybe I should say something to the kid's parents. Suggest that her father sit behind Mr. Big there, so the little girl can see the game."

Billy didn't respond. He just sat quietly watching the players go through their warm-up drills.

"I know the game hasn't started, but when it does, she won't be able to see through that wall of blubber in front of her."

"Okay, tell them," Billy said challengingly, looking directly into Charlie's eyes.

So Billy was daring him to go up to the kid's parents and say something! Okay, he would. He stood up and moved past Billy toward the aisle. With some difficulty, he maneuvered his way between knees and backs down to the second row where the little girl sat between her parents. He stopped abruptly and then turned and looked sheepishly at Billy. As Billy pulled the collar of his leather jacket snugly around his neck, a grin spread over his face. He nodded to Charlie to proceed. Charlie felt the hot flush of blood against his cheeks. He squeezed his way down the row toward the couple and the little girl, bumping against a few knees along the way.

"Hey, Charlie," said a deep voice. "I thought it was you I saw you pull up on a motorcycle."

It was Pat Brixton. Charlie sat two seats behind him in history class. Pat played linebacker on the school's football team. Charlie looked down at Pat, whose black ski cap was in his lap clamped between his thick legs. Pat's buddy sat next to him sipping a Coke and chomping on a Baby Ruth candy bar. Pat was the largest kid in the junior class. He wasn't just tall. He was wide. His shoulders were so broad that at times Charlie couldn't see around him to the front board. Of course, he rarely needed to, since Coach Wilkins wasn't in the habit of using it.

"Yeah, Billy and I rode over to check out the game."

"You two gonna freeze your gonads off on a night like this. Bikes are for summer, man."

"No, bikes are for ridin'."

24

"And for pickin' up chicks," said the guy next to Pat. Charlie didn't know him very well. He was a new student at school, and judging by his size another candidate for membership in the school's jock club. His pimply face was broken out all over in blotchy red patches. He looked like he had slept face down in a poison ivy patch. Charlie couldn't help noticing three pus-filled pimples, ripe for squeezing, on his right cheek. Coach Wilkins hadn't wasted any time recruiting him and already had him sitting in one of the front-row seats. Thank God, Charlie thought: at least, if he had to sit next to him in history, he only had to look at the back of his head.

"Speakin' of chicks, Charlie, is Billy boy gettin' any from Praxy?"

"Now she's real classy stuff," the new kid blurted out.

"Especially the way her hard little nipples rub up against those thin sweaters she wears to school," chuckled the acne-faced kid, unabashedly squeezing one of the large pimples on the side of his cheek. "Now that's class."

"Billy boy's sittin' right up there," Charlie said, pointing four rows up. "Why not ask him? Maybe he'd get a laugh or two out of your cute joke about Praxy's breasts. Or maybe he'd just tell you to screw off."

"Praxy's breasts. Listen to you. What's this breast shit, Charlie? You mean her tits, her boobs, her knockers, her bazookas, not her breasts, man. Breasts! You sound like a flake. And personally, dude, you can tell him whatever you like. And while you're at it, you can tell him that I don't see what Praxy sees in a greaser like him anyway. The guy's a loser. He comes to school whenever he feels like it. Doesn't give a shit about his grades, sleeps through most of his classes, and has never even played a school sport. Just thinks he's Mr. Cool or something. Piss on him! If you want to hang out with him, that's your business, but don't ask for any sympathy."

"Sympathy! What the fuck are you talking about!" Charlie screamed. He was furious. The little girl jumped a foot or so out of her seat, grabbed her mother's arm, and buried her face in the folds of her coat. Her parents turned around, their faces livid, as they stared at him in disbelief.

God! This is simply absurd, he thought. He had gotten into this mess because he felt sorry for the little girl. Now she was frightened to death of him. And everybody was gawking at him like he was some kind of mental case, everyone except the walrus. The walrus just sat there feeding his face, completely unmoved by Charlie's sudden outburst.

Charlie turned around and looked at Billy. He had stood up and was moving toward the aisle. Charlie felt ridiculous. He just wanted to get out of there. To hell with the basketball game. How could things get so fouled up? Why couldn't he have just ignored these two bozos? They were only trying to be funny in their own moronic way. Christ's sake, it was only a stupid remark! They couldn't care less about Billy or Praxy. An innocent tit joke, Charlie thought, and then he had to go and say something really pathetic. The way he had handled it!

Who in the hell ever uses the word "breasts" anyway? He was just asking to be called weird.

"Look," Charlie said timorously, forcing himself to take control, "Why don't we just forget it? You choose your friends, and I'll choose mine." He paused for a few seconds, watching the Blob take another candy out of his pocket, and then he tapped him lightly on the shoulder. "You're blocking this little girl's view," he mumbled. And then turning to her parents, he said, softly, apologetically, "The kid can't see the game. Maybe the three of you can work something out." Charlie made his way past Pat and his friend and back into the aisle.

Billy had moved down from above and now stood, his hands shoved in his pockets, in front of Charlie. He had an incredulous look on his face. "What was that all about? Christ, I thought you came here because you wanted to see the friggin' game," he said, removing a comb from his rear pocket and smoothing back his wavy brown ducktails. "Man, what did you say to those two clowns?" he chuckled, nodding in the direction of Pat Brixton and his buddy.

"Nothing, man. Just forget it," Charlie said. "Do we still have our places?"

"I think so. What happened anyway?"

"I said forget it. It was stupid. I should have just let the whole thing alone." Suddenly Charlie shot a glance past Billy to the rear corner of the gym. "Guess who just popped in?" He waved in the direction of the side door where Praxy and her father were standing looking for empty seats.

Praxy waved back excitedly while her father only returned a cursory wave and then began looking for a spot on the far side of the gym.

In that brief moment of their distant exchange, Charlie noticed Praxy's surprise and then embarrassment over her father's effort to distance himself. She had once told Charlie that her father had this problem with her dating a guy who rode a motorcycle. But that wasn't it exactly. After all, Charlie had a motorcycle too.

"Doesn't look like her old man wants to sit near us. Think we should join them anyway?" Billy said half-jokingly.

"Are you kiddin'? Besides, we have better seats right here."

"You afraid of him?"

"Not really. He's okay, once you get to know him. Maybe a bit too protective when it comes to Praxy," Charlie laughed, "but not a bad guy. He plays golf with my father occasionally. I sometimes go along and caddie for them. Mr. Bishop always gives me a big tip."

"Protective isn't the word. Paranoid's more like it," Billy said, reentering the row where they had been sitting.

"He's just cautious, that's all. Your typical father worried about his daughter's welfare."

"Worried? Is there any reason why he should be? Maybe it's the company she's keeping."

"Hey, I don't know. If you ask me, the company's fine." Charlie wasn't clear on what Billy wanted out of him. He was beginning to regret having said anything.

"Look, man, I don't really give a big hoot what he thinks about me. But I think she's old enough to choose her own friends, even if they're high school dropouts."

"High school dropouts? You're hardly a high school dropout. God, you take this all too personally. Really."

"How am I friggin' supposed to take it if it concerns me? Be serious. The guy gets whacked out of shape if she goes to a race with me? Man, we're not Hell's Angels taking her to a gang banging. I like racing motorcycles. That doesn't make me a degenerate." He paused. "Though it does look like it's going to make me a high school dropout."

"What's this dropout stuff?"

"It's like this, pal. If I make Expert before March, and according to my calculations I think I already have, then I'll be goin' for national points mostly. National points means followin' the national circuit. And that means beaucoup travellin', startin' with Daytona in March."

"You're serious? When will you find out about your points?"

"I'm waiting to hear from the AMA office in Westerville. I should be gettin' a letter any day."

"So, you're really gonna do it?" Charlie wondered how Praxy would receive the news. "Where are you gonna get the money? I mean, to race around? Most guys on the circuit have factory sponsors, don't they?

"No, not really. Harley-Davidson's only sponsoring two riders. And Honda about the same. The rest are pretty much privateers with shops footin' the bill. Bradley's Harley-Davidson is backing me right now, and

Tom says that if I want to compete on the circuit, he'll help me. He knows that I won't be able to work much at the shop on the weekends to pay him back, but he says that's okay. All I got to do is win a few big races, and he'll get paid back in advertising. While I'm travelin' between races, he'll pick up the cost of motels: that is as long as I don't stay at the Holiday Inn or the Sheraton."

Charlie could feel the tension in the air as the din in the gym died down to a hushed silence. Down below, the game was about to begin. The referee stepped over to the circle of players at center court, holding the game ball high over his head. The two centers, hands at their sides, knees bent slightly, eagled in on the ball. Hundreds of eyes locked on the players and on the referee. Then all that could be heard was the shrill sound of the whistle as he tossed the ball a meter over the centers' heads.

McKinley's center leaped an inch or two higher than Oak Creek's and tipped the ball to his point guard. The guard passed the ball down court to the forward, who charged into the key for an easy layup. The crowd exploded. Charlie was out of his seat screaming, "Go McKinley!" Then the clamor died down some as Oak Creek, in possession of the ball, moved it down court. Charlie averted his eyes from the game for a few seconds to catch Billy's reaction. He was studying the moves of the players like Charlie had seen him study riders out on the racetrack during practice sessions.

Charlie felt juvenile. Billy could make him feel like that. A moment ago they were discussing what could be the most important decision of Billy's life. And now he was acting like a cheerleader, jumping out of his seat and heehawing. Okay, so basketball worked him up. What was wrong with that? After all, there was a lot to the game, if you knew how it was played and were a team player. Now Billy, he wasn't a team player. That's probably why the game didn't do that much for him. Billy wasn't ever likely to be on anyone's team, and goons like Pat Brixton saw that right away. Yet he was an athlete. There was no doubt about that. Thundering down the straightaway at 130 miles per hour and into a turn sideways at over a 100, with the ground whizzing by under you, no doubt took exceptional composure and natural athletic ability. And maybe, Charlie reflected, a small measure of lunacy.

For Billy, motorcycle racing was more than a sport. It was a kind of religion, his raison d'être. A word his English teacher always used in class to describe her love for teaching literature. The next few years of his life would be spent kneeling at the altar of his god. And in dropping out of school, he was about to undergo his baptismal. And why not? Charlie thought wistfully. At least there was something alive inside stirring him. And as for himself, what moved him? At this point in his life, he had nothing to dedicate himself to. He was a sideliner, like Praxy's father, a spectator at a weekend basketball game. At best only vicariously playing the athlete. Without his consent or approval, his future had somehow already been laid out for him in bold type. He would graduate from a respectable high school with respectable grades, be accepted into a respectable college in the boring Midwest, pursue a respectable career, marry a respectable woman, and raise a respectable family. That about said it all.

In the school parking lot outside the gym, headlights crisscrossed each other like neon batons flung high in the night air by a bunch of frenzied high school band members. Charlie spotted Praxy standing with her father next to their car. He shouted out to her, trying to make her hear him above the honking horns that celebrated McKinley's win.

"Come on, man, let's take a cruise down Hampton Road," Billy said dryly. "Mr. Bishop needs to take his daughter home. Make sure she's safe and sound."

He and Billy had taken several late-night cruises down Hampton Road. Hampton Road wound in and out of a wooded stretch of land that spread thirty miles north through the greater part of Bathside County. By early evening, the road became as empty as a hobo's pockets. In the summer months, the large elm and maple trees lining the road launched their long thin limbs over the asphalt pavement. As the temperature fell in the evening, warm air trapped by the earth and asphalt would collect at intervals along this long stretch of country road, creating a thermal tunnel. On summer nights Charlie and Billy enjoyed surfing the thermals, thick tepid chambers of warm moist air trapped in the conduit of country road that lay under the arching trees.

"You comin' or stayin'?" Billy said, pulling Charlie out of his momentary reverie.

"Just thought maybe we'd say hello to Praxy and her dad. He must be really pumped over the game. We're regional champs now!" he yelled out, trying to raise Billy's spirits. "Anyway, it looks like she's expecting us to go over and say hi."

Praxy leaned her back against the hood of her father's car, her arms folded patiently in front of her. Mr. Bishop had already opened the driver's door and was waiting for her to go around to the other side. Praxy smiled, waiting for them to cross the parking lot.

"Yeah, okay," Billy said reluctantly. "I'd rather just call her later though."

"Hi, Praxy! Hello, Mr. Bishop. Enjoyed the game, I bet," Charlie said, shaking hands with Praxy's father and then absentmindedly rubbing his hands up and down the front of his thighs. He noticed her father staring at his teeth. Reflexively, he lifted his fingers to his mouth and felt the sharp edge of his incisors. "Looks like our Tigers plucked the Falcon's feathers," he said and then laughed uneasily, embarrassed by his silly metaphor.

Billy stood there with his shoulders hunched and the wool collar of his black leather jacket pulled up around his neck. His eyes alternated between the packed limestone gravel at his feet and Praxy. "Hi," Billy mumbled, awkwardly extending his hand to her father. And then turning to Praxy, "Hi, Praxy." He kicked a couple of stones loose with the toe of his boot and then shoved his hands back into the pockets of his blue jeans.

Charlie couldn't help but notice this attitude thing Billy broadcasted to Mr. Bishop. Whether it was intentional or not, he couldn't be sure. Nonetheless, Billy gave the unequivocal impression that he was about as interested in small talk with Bishop as Hitler would have been discussing the '38 Olympics with a convocation of rabbis.

"I didn't know you were a basketball fan, Billy."

"I'm not, really. I've played some hoops now and then after school with Charlie and a couple of the guys. I like the game all right, but I guess I'm not crazy about it."

"Praxy tells me you're a professional motorcycle racer. I guess with school and racing, you wouldn't have a whole lot of time to come to many of the games on the weekend anyway."

"If Billy gets his Expert points," Charlie said, "he's going to compete on the national circuit. His first race will be in March at Daytona Beach. If I can talk my parents into it, I'd like to go down there with him."

"Wouldn't you have to miss school?" There was this strong paternal ring in Mr. Bishop's voice.

"Well, he could just come down for the stadium race," Billy interjected. "That's the big race. After the national, there are only a couple of pro races in the area that pay anything, and then most of the riders head out to the West Coast for the mile race in Pamona."

"And what would you do about school, that is if you plan to race on the circuit, as you say?"

"I guess it would have to wait."

"Oh, I see. And how much does the winner of one of these Nationals make?" her father asked rather pointedly.

"Well, I'm not sure. I think about fifteen thousand."

"Fifteen thousand? For first place?"

"Yeah, something like that."

"How many Nationals does the average pro racer win a year?"

"The average pro racer? None."

"I see," Mr. Bishop said curtly. "And you plan to go to Daytona this spring and race in one of these Nationals?"

"I'm hoping to," Billy said.

Charlie watched Billy's eyes fix on Praxy. He realized now that Billy hadn't said anything to her about his recent career plans. She looked apprehensive and confused. A thin white line formed against her lower lip as she bit down on it sharply.

Charlie couldn't take his thoughts off how beautiful she was standing there in the soft light. Her face seemed to absorb all the moonlight, and the circle of light in which the four of them stood seemed visible by her glow alone. Her blond hair fell in tendrils across her brow and in rebellious twisting and wiry ringlets onto the collar of her gray windbreaker. His eyes traveled downward to the symmetrical swells under her beige windbreaker. Suddenly he thought about the incident with Pat Brixton and became angry all over again. Brixton would probably grow up to be a serial rapist. Brixton had only one thing on his mind. And the funny thing was the guy had probably never seen a real naked woman except on a porno Internet site or at the movies. Well, neither had he for that matter, except once, and by accident, when his mother passed in a cloud of steam from the bathroom to her bedroom.

And now as he looked at Praxy and at the upward curve of her breasts pressing against the light fabric of her windbreaker, he had this powerful adolescent stirring of desire, followed instantly by a sharp prick of guilt. In the cool night air, his thoughts moved sullenly, like an errant, contrite child, from her to Billy, and an ineffable feeling welled up inside him.

Billy took his leather gloves out of his side pockets and slipped them on while he looked around the parking lot, set on avoiding any further words with her father.

"Well, honey, I think we should be going."

"Yeah, sure, Dad. Bye, guys." Her voice was tight and forced, barely audible.

"Good night, gentlemen," Mr. Bishop said, and then bent down and edged his tall, thin frame inside the car.

"I'll call you tomorrow," Billy said tentatively, watching Praxy open the door and sink down into the pale yellow light of the interior. When Mr. Bishop slammed the door shut, Praxy disappeared, swallowed up in the darkness behind the shiny opaque windows of the car.

The warm air rushing in through the small opening above the window lifted Praxy's hair and parted her bangs. *I'll call you tomorrow.* The words turned over and over again like chopped cabbage in a blender. So, tomorrow he'd tell her about his future plans.

"You enjoyed the game?" her father asked.

"Yeah, Dad. I sure did. It was great. I can't believe we're in the state finals." Her reply was a bit too casual and distant to be convincing. *I'll call you tomorrow.* What was he going to say?

36

It was funny. She had grown up in a family where planning for the future entailed attending college. And not just any old college, but a private one. This meant getting good grades in high school and doing well on SATs. And now she was dating a soon-to-be high school dropout. What would it be like when she went away to college? And where would Billy be? He'd be somewhere on the road— Oklahoma, Texas, Florida, only Harley-Davidson knew where…

"Well, what's your boyfriend majoring in?"

"He's into grease and chains and the smell of high-octane fossil fuel. And leather, of course. Yes, leather. He wears a lot of leather."

"You don't say. He sounds real punk. Wow, cool, leather's real rad."

"Yeah every Saturday and Sunday he dresses out in the coolest leatherwear from toe to fingertip. You see, it's a requirement of his profession, like a lab jacket is for a lab technician."

"Oh, he works with dangerous chemicals. I guessed it— chemical engineering. He's going to be a chemical engineer?"

"Well, the truth is, girls, he…well he…how can I say this to communicate the fullness and the glory of his calling? Yes, I have it. He's a kind of modern knight. That's it. A modern knight on horseback. And his job is to make his stallion go faster around the track than any of the competing knights' stallions."

"Gee, it sounds real exciting. And romantic, whatever it is that he does. Will he make a lot of money at it?"

"Money? Money? Why, no. That's not the point! It's not about that at all. You see, his plans are to…"

"Praxy, you know I have always tried to be the kind of father who meddled as little as possible in your personal affairs, but I feel compelled now to say something about you... and Billy."

He was speaking in that biblical voice again, like the hoary old Abraham. Praxy's blood froze.

"Honey, you know I love you," he continued, reaching over and touching her arm, "and what I'm about to say might upset you, but I feel that I have to say it."

She would not give in. She loved him, too, but loving your father didn't mean you had to betray your own feelings. *Whoso would be a man must be a non-conformist.* Sometimes being truthful with those you love meant possibly hurting them. Unless being a hypocrite didn't bother you.

"I don't want you getting overly involved with someone like Billy. I prefer that you don't see him outside of school."

There it was. The papal decree, Praxy thought. She stared silently out the side window into the darkness whizzing by.

"It's not the motorcycles, though you know how I feel about motorcycles. Charlie has a motorcycle, and if you want to go out with him, fine. It's just that Billy's chosen a path in life that I think...that I think...is incompatible with your future happiness."

"Incompatible with my future happiness?"

"Yes, Praxy, incompatible."

"I don't understand. Is it about college? Is that it?"

"Praxy, honey, Billy might not even finish high school. Do you know what that means? I'm not trying to tell you who you should choose as your boyfriend, but…"

"You're not trying to tell me who to choose as my boyfriend? Then what are you saying? Look, I know Billy isn't your average high school student, but don't you think he deserves a chance? Many great people never finished college. Did you know that? Shakespeare had what was equivalent to a grammar school education. And Steve Jobs only attended college for a semester! So why is it important that Billy finish high school right now? He can finish later. Even if he doesn't, even if he drops out tomorrow and gets a job at McDonald's, would that really change who he is? Must a person be what you want, Dad?" She paused and then said bitterly, "Would you be happier if I had a boyfriend who was planning to become a dentist?"

"Praxy," he said, reaching over to brush back a long, curly strand of hair that hung down over her forehead. She drew her head away from his outstretched hand and leaned it against the side window. "I'm not saying that he is a loser. I'm not saying that he is anything, but he made it clear enough tonight after the game that he most likely won't finish high school."

"He could take night classes in the winter, once the racing season is over. And even if he never goes back to school, why should that bar him from my company or anyone's? Billy isn't a loser, Dad. He's bright and thinks about things. He knows who he is and what he wants out of life, and that makes him a heck of a lot more mature than most teenagers my age. And besides, he's talented at what he loves. He's one of the best motorcycle racers in the entire state, and he's only eighteen."

"It's not just that he might become a dropout. There's more to it than that. Look at his home life. I've asked around about his family. His mother works on the assembly line at Markheim Rubber Products. She dropped out of school when she was sixteen and has worked as a waitress or a factory laborer most of her life. And his father disappeared after Billy's eleventh birthday. He left his children and his wife for a younger woman, a bartender."

"Their father died of a stroke last year. Did you research that too?"

"I heard. And what's his brother doing now?"

"His brother went to the funeral and afterwards decided to stay out West."

"Stay and do what?"

"Stay and work on cars. Billy says he's a great mechanic."

"A mechanic? Don't you see, Praxy? That's what the family's about. I want more for you than that. I've seen it all my life. Children acquire their parents' dispositions and tendencies. It's a rare kid who can break the iron bands of family upbringing and genes."

"But people are individuals, not clones. Billy is as different from his brother as I am…as I am from you. Sure we share some similar ideas, but we are not the same. Kids are not the same as their parents. What makes them the same are narrow-minded interpretations imposed on them by people who don't believe in…I don't know…who don't believe in…freedom."

40

"In freedom? Come on, Praxy. What does any of this have to do with freedom?"

"It has everything to do with freedom, Dad. Billy can be what he wants to be. He's not his father or his brother, or his mother, for that matter. He might have their genes, but a person is more than genes. Sure they might look alike, share a certain family resemblance, but he is Billy, just as I am Praxy. Dad, give him a chance. I know what I'm doing. If you really love me, have faith in me."

"I do love you, honey. It's just that I want what's best for you. That's all."

Praxy listened to the night air whistle through the small opening at the top of the car window. The muscles in her neck had tightened from the stream of frigid air rushing past her face and down her neck. She thought of winding the window up, but the sound of the air comforted her. It helped deaden the sound of her father's stinging, sententious words that still echoed through the small compartment of the car. She wanted more than anything for the wind rushing through the crack to suck them into its slipstream and carry them out the window and loose them forever to the swirling darkness.

CHAPTER FOUR

Today started out horribly with the friggin' Stockton incident and the pills and all. And then later the lightheadedness and passing out. I told Phillips about the fainting spell, asked him if it had anything to do with the pills I'm taking. He didn't answer me directly but wanted to know what happened right before the rush came over me. I told him that I couldn't remember anything clearly. The last thing I could recall was something vague about our jackets, Charlie's and mine. He wanted to know more about the jackets. I told him Charlie had bought a leather jacket right after he got his Honda. He asked me if it was an aviation jacket. Yeah, I told him. I wonder how he knew. Anyway, I told him that it happened all of a sudden. WHAM! I felt dizzier than hell. And short of breath, like someone had smacked me in the chest with a two-by-four. He asked me to tell him about the jackets, anything I could remember about them. He thought it might have something to do with the passing out business.

Well, the damn thing is I couldn't remember a thing. Jesus, it makes me think I'm wacko. When I tried to recall any details about the jackets, I drew a huge blank. I tried like hell to remember, to focus my thoughts on the jackets. After a few minutes, my head began to pound like it was an empty oil drum and someone was striking the drum with a tire iron. I couldn't remember any details about the jackets, how many pockets they had, whether they had straps, wide lapels, buckles, stars, or what.

When I told Phillips about it, he said that not being able to remember was normal, and in time everything would come back to me. But I had to keep trying to remember things, even painful things. Then he said, with this phony air of confidence, that he wanted to help me, but wanting to help me wouldn't be enough. I had to help me, too. No shit. Like it doesn't take a fifty-dollar an hour analyst to figure that out.

I'd like to trust him. Or trust someone. But who? Certainly not that lummox Stockton. Before I confide in anyone, I need to know more. Something about Phillips gives me the creeps. Until I figure it out, trusting him will help me about as much as an extra lock on the door. Or another Stockton to cram pills down my throat. Phillips just isn't leveling with me. His meetings seem more like undercover work than therapy, if that's what our little get-togethers are supposed to be.

"Why am I being kept against my will?" I ask.

"It's in your best interests," he tells me.

Now what kind of answer is that? Does that sound like it's coming from a person who gives a shit? In my best interests? "Guess not seeing my parents is in my best interests too?" I ask him. "And the locks on the doors, those are in my best interests also?"

"Your mother has already visited you," he tells me.

Icy fingers crawl over my skin, and his voice seems faraway, coming from the depths of some vast underground cavern.

"Why, that's a lie!" I tell him.

"No, it's not a lie," he says.

"If it's true, then why don't I remember it?"

"She came to see you right after you were brought here." His words bounce off the sides of the cavern, resonating, backfiring, like an engine out of time.

"Brought here? Brought here from where?"

"From downtown. You had been picked up outside of Tom Bradley's Harley-Davidson shop."

The noise grows louder. The words are less discrete, like backfires exploding from the exhaust pipes of a dozen out-of-tune Harleys.

"You were brought here to sort things out," he assures me. "You seem to be mixed up about a number of things. That's why we're administering the sedatives."

"And the drugs, or sedatives as you call them, are supposed to help me remember?" I laugh at the irony of it. I think about all the silly propaganda at school, the special assemblies with guest speakers preaching about crack mothers, heroin addicts, and cocaine suicides. And now, I'm being force-fed drugs so I can remember things, so I can recover.

"You shouldn't think of them as drugs, but as medicine," he tells me. "They will help you recall some important things, though the treatment might take some time."

"So they're supposed to get me to recall things. Is that it? Okay!" I tell him. I have to shout to be heard above the clamor of our dizzying words. "Fine! You want me to cooperate? Then I expect the same!" I scream. "I expect the goddamn same! Let me talk to Charlie," I say suddenly, unexpectedly. "I need to see him. He will help me straighten things out." Charlie is the answer. I know he is. He's the welding rod needed to fuse things together again.

"That's impossible right now!" he shouts back, trying to reach me above the exploding exhaust. "Later you'll see Charlie," he answers with a placating smile, his voice fainter now.

"When?" I ask, holding my hands tightly against my temples.

"That depends on you," he says. His words are drowned out, lost in the powerful storm of over-revved engines. "That depends on you."

Then the kill-switch buttons are pushed and the clamor of engines dies, the storm abates. Followed by dead silence, silence as still and lifeless as twisted metal wrapped around tree bark. I sit there, numb, holding my head in my hands.

After dinner I get a surprise visit. Rarely does Phillips wish to see me twice on the same day. He wants to know if I feel like talking.

"About what?" I ask him.

He suggests that I talk about Charlie, about our friendship, how we met, stuff like that. I tell him that I met Charlie through Praxy. They were close friends, used to be neighbors even. Charlie has a Honda CX 500. Sometimes, when the weather was nice, he would pass by Praxy's house and give her a lift to school.

"Did Charlie have a girlfriend?" he asks me. I tell him I don't remember Charlie ever dating anyone, except one time when Praxy fixed him up with her cousin. Kind of a double date. We took them for a ride on our bikes, out in the country to a special place where Charlie and I and sometimes Praxy go. It's a great place to just sit around and shoot the breeze. You have to travel about a quarter of a mile or so down this dirt road. Then there's a narrow, rocky path that leads down a hill to a pond. We'd park our bikes on top of this wooded hill and walk down the steep path to the pond. The pond has a rock cliff on one of its banks with a flat thin strip of shore at its base. We'd sometimes go skinny dipping there, Praxy included. But with our underwear on.

"And how did you and Praxy become friends?" he wants to know.

I tell Phillips that I had two classes with her, history and English. I got to know her one day in history class. History class. My thoughts about that class are about as pleasant as my thoughts about going to the dentist to get a tooth yanked. No doubt, history was my least favorite class, but not because I don't like history. I probably know as much about history as Coach Wilkins. Which doesn't say a lot. I suspect he knows about enough to pass an immigrant citizenship test. And that's probably giving him too much credit. Well, it was the goon squad and Coach Wilkins, the ape trainer, that helped sour me on history. In class, his thick-necked simians would sit in the front row, like trained circus animals, drooling in self-flattery whenever he compared football and football players to events in history. History was nothing to him but generals leading their men to the playoffs. Or if they were great generals, like Lee or MacArthur, to the Super

Bowl. When I think about it, which is rarely, I don't know if I'm more amused or amazed.

And to look at Coach Wilkins, you would guess he was anything but an athlete. Maybe a truck driver or some dumpy used car salesman who sat around all day on his fat can. His body makes Danny De Vito's look like the god Apollo. He's about five ten, weighs about what a fifty-gallon barrel of axle grease weighs, is neckless, and is shaped like a fishing bobber, only his head is slightly less pointed.

Anyway, I tell Phillips I had been in his friggin' class for nearly a semester and hadn't said a word to Praxy. I had certainly noticed her though. She sat one seat back and to the left of me in the row closest to the window. Her curly blond hair, which frizzes out in these wild, crazy directions, drove me absolutely crazy. I would pretend to look out the window so I could catch a furtive glimpse of her. Her nose turns slightly upwards like the front fender of an old Indian motorcycle, like the one the guardian angel road in that old movie *Kid Celestial*. And her lips are as full and sensuous and red as a strawberry heavy with summer dew.

In class one Friday, Wilkins assigned some end-of-the-chapter questions for us, while his Neanderthal brain worked on one of his weekly sports schedules. The questions were the kind that you could answer in about fifteen minutes, if you had half a brain, but he made it a point to give us the whole period. His goons probably needed it. I had scribbled some stupid stuff down, knowing he never looked at homework anyway. Then I took an issue of *Cycle* magazine out of my backpack under my desk. I had brought the magazine from home. It was the latest issue, and it happened to cover the dirt track National at Louisville.

A few minutes into reading the article on the Louisville Half-mile, I glanced up and caught Praxy looking at a picture of Scot Parker, the National Number One plate holder.

I explain to Phillips that the National Number One is the guy with the most National points at the end of the season. In this photo of Parker, he is shown in a power slide, his front wheel crossed up, and his bike sideways, thundering through a turn at Louisville's half-mile track.

Anyway, I remember our eyes intercepting each other and her smiling and pointing, first to me, and then to the magazine. "Do you do this?" she asked, those beautiful lips of hers silently forming the question.

I couldn't believe it. How did she know I raced motorcycles? I grinned back, and moving my mouth silently formed the words, "Yes, but not as well."

I guess she must have thought my answer was pretty funny because she immediately put her hands over her mouth and tried to keep herself from laughing, but two low snickers shot through her fingers. They were loud enough to catch the attention of some of Wilkins's wildebeests that sat directly in front of us, and then Wilkins. Two of them turned around, flashing apish grins, while Wilkins slowly floated up from his desk like a fat canal carp surfacing from an open sewer.

I shut the magazine, flipped open my history book, and slid it on top of the magazine. It didn't work. The history book was smaller than the magazine. Wilkins lumbered over to my desk and put his meaty finger down on the edge of the magazine, holding it in place, and with his other hand he pushed the history book roughly to the side.

"What's this, Solinski?" He pronounced it sky instead of ski.

"It's last month's issue of *Cycle*."

"Does it have anything in it about World War I?"

"I don't know, Mr. Wilkins. I haven't finished reading it."

"Mr. Wilkins," spurted out Clinton, his right-hand ape, "that magazine he's got don't have nothin' in it but pretty pitchures of motorsicles with guys with faggot-type Elvis Presley hairdo's." This was followed immediately by a roar of laughter that sounded like a herd of mating moose.

"Okay, Clinton, let me handle this, all right?" Wilkins said, bringing his beasts under control. The laughter ended as suddenly as it had begun.

"One issue I read did have a piece on World War I army bikes, some old Indians and Henderson's. They were great bikes, used for mail delivery and…"

"That's interesting, SolinSKY, but I don't think anything about motorsickles," he turned, his two cold eyes on Praxy, "will help any of you on the chapter quiz tomorrow."

"The chapter quiz! Come on, coach!" his wildebeests mooed sorrowfully. You would think that someone had stolen their Super Bowl passes.

Not saying a word more, Wilkins snatched up the magazine and wallowed back to his desk.

49

"Shit, Solinski," moaned Clinton, twisting his small bullet head around on that stubby neck of his. As he swung it around, I imagined the sound of a screeching, ungreased fork bearing. "Now look what you did."

"I did it just for you, Clinton. You need to study. You know why?" I whispered. "Because you'll need to know more about life than how to put on your jockstrap, if you ever graduate from high school, that is. And, you know, Wilkins won't always be there to strap you in."

I remember Clinton's pink cheeks reddening while he mumbled under his breath some incoherent remark about fags and motorcycles. I thought Praxy was going to split her pants trying to hold back her laughter. Fortunately, the bell saved her.

"You want to join me and a friend for lunch?" she asked in this buoyant voice of hers.

"It depends. Who's the friend? If it's Clinton, forget it."

"Give me more credit than that," she laughed.

"Just checkin' you out, that's all."

She stood there in the hall for what seemed like an incredibly long time, but in reality was probably just a few seconds. She held her books tightly against her, and her eyes kept looking searchingly into mine. It made me feel a bit uneasy, like my stomach was full of ants and taco sauce.

"Yeah, and what do you see?" she asked playfully.

"I'm not sure."

I remember my eyes moving downward to her books. She had them squeezed firmly against her breasts. My eyes lingered there for about a second or two. I kept thinking, a little embarrassedly, how I would like to trade places with the books. And then kind of fumbling, digging for something, anything to say, I asked her if she liked motorcycles.

"Sure. A friend of mine has a Honda. He's in your U.S. Government class."

"By the way, how did you know I raced motorcycles?"

"My friend told me."

"Your friend?"

"Yeah, I'll introduce you two at lunch, if you want, that is? What do you say?" she said, shifting her books around some while looking at me wistfully.

"Sure. See you in the cafeteria."

Suddenly, as I'm about to conclude telling Phillips about Praxy, I have this floating sensation and feel a little dizzy like I just inhaled some high-octane fumes.

Phillips doesn't notice. He asks me if I met Charlie that same day. Yeah, I tell him. Praxy introduced us. Then he asks me what my impression of Charlie was.

All of a sudden I'm tired. I tell him I don't feel like talking anymore. I suggest we continue tomorrow. Apparently he can see that I am tired, and so he agrees.

51

CHAPTER FIVE

"Hello, Praxy?"

It was Billy. She had been waiting by the phone for his call, hoping, if he did call, to snatch up the phone before her father answered it. It was about ten-thirty and the temperature had fallen to near freezing. She sat at the head of her bed, her back resting on the oak headboard. Though her room was warm and cozy, cold air from outside nestled against the window beside her bed. She moved her hand playfully in front of the windowpane and felt its coolness against her open palm.

"Billy, are you really going to do it?" A shiver passed down her neck and over her shoulders.

"You mean about school?"

"Yes."

"I said if I got my points I would. I already have a shop that will sponsor me fully."

She waited.

"And it's not easy to get sponsors. If I pass up this opportunity, then I might not get another shot at it."

"And graduating? Do you have any plans about that?" Her question sounded odd. It startled her. It was the kind of question her father would ask.

"It depends."

"It depends on what?"

"It depends on what I do on the national circuit. If I think I have a chance, then I'll stay with it. And if not, I'll probably go back to school, maybe night school, or study to pass the G.E.D."

"Then what? Join the army?" She cringed, like she was expecting a sharp jab. Slowly, she told herself. Not so fast. You're trespassing on private ground with off-limits signs posted all around its borders.

"I don't know. If everything else fails, maybe I'll become a dentist or something, you know, clean and pull teeth for a living."

She had done it, crossed the boundary. He had a right to be offended. Okay, she had to take control now. She couldn't let herself be stung by his words. She had asked for it anyway. Now she simply had to extricate herself before things took an even worse turn.

"Well, Billy, maybe my father would take you on as a partner. The two of you could set up shop together." The thought of Billy as a dentist made her laugh. Billy as a dentist. He would look about as funny as her father in a black leather jacket—riding to his office on a full-dress Harley.

"Yeah, and maybe I could talk him into buying a Honda Gold Wing, and we could ride together to the annual dentist conventions. You know, stay at all those swank hotels, like the Sheraton and the Ramada Inn."

He was okay now.

"My exact thoughts," she laughed. "But I was thinking more along the lines of a Harley-Davidson. You know, one of those big jobs with fiberglass boxes hanging off the sides and with more lights than a Christmas tree." She bent forward, picked up an issue of

People magazine from the foot of her bed, and began flipping through it.

But what would Billy do if racing did turn out to be a dead end? Would he hang on at Bradley's? Repairing motorcycles? Changing spark plugs and doing tune-ups? And if it did come down to that? Was replacing spark plugs really any different than filling cavities and fitting someone for braces?

"So you like those fancy hogs?" he chuckled. "I thought your tastes were more refined. BMWs maybe?"

"That's what I get for hangin' around with the likes of you."

It was true. She couldn't refrain from judging him. Just like my father, she thought. And only a little while before *she* was telling *him* he needed to give Billy a chance. Maybe her father was right. Maybe children are just like their parents. Regardless of how determined they are to be themselves.

"The likes of me? I have an old Triumph, not a full-dress Harley. And you know, that old bike suits me just fine."

"Hey, I know it suits you fine. It's a classy bike. Why wouldn't it?"

"So, you think I have class? Would dating a dropout be a problem for you?

"Not if you weren't bothered by it." She wasn't sure how convincing she sounded. But then why did she need to sound convincing?

"Well, every person has to find his own groove. That's how I see it. And I've found mine. You see, Praxy, I know what I want."

"And me, do you think I know what I want?" she asked, feeling the need for some reassurance.

"Sure. You know. Everyone does. If they can just push the crap aside."

"Billy, I hope you get your points. And if you do, high school can wait," she said, her finger tracing the outline of a fancy dress in the magazine.

"Thanks, Praxy. It's good to hear that. And promise me something, okay?"

"Sure."

"Promise me you won't be too disappointed if I don't make the final at Daytona."

"The final at Daytona?" she asked, closing the magazine.

He hesitated and then said jokingly, "Maybe you can talk your parents into letting you go to Florida for the weekend."

"You sound like you're already packing. Billy, are you holding back? Is there something you're not telling me?"

"You won't believe this, but tonight when I got home from the friggin' game, my mother had this surprise for me. She handed me a letter from the AMA office in Westerville."

"A letter?"

"Yes, a letter. I'm officially an Expert professional motorcycle racer."

"Billy! I don't believe it! You're kidding? Why, this is great! Did you tell Charlie?"

"No, he'd gone on home. You're the first one I've talked to since I read the letter. They even let me keep my old number, 12F. All I need to do is change the color of the number plates from yellow to white. And if everything goes well this year, next year I drop the letter."

"Why's that?"

"I'll be a National Number."

"You'll drop the F?" she asked.

"National Numbers don't have letters following their numbers. That's because they're National Numbers!" His voice sounded like that of an elementary school teacher lecturing to some little kids. "See what I mean?"

"Well, yeah, I guess, but…"

"National Numbers are given to the top 100 Expert racers in the country. It's based on their points standings in competitions. The reason the letter isn't necessary is because they are no longer local boys associated with any one part of the country."

"So, this Sunday at the in-door race in Detroit, you'll have a chance to get Expert points?

"No, I can pick up Expert points only at events where I compete against other Experts only."

"Oh," she said. "So after the indoor race this weekend, when's your next Expert race, not National, but regular race?"

"Next Saturday night, in Valdosta, Georgia.

"So you're really going to Florida? God, Billy, I can't believe it!"

"I know. I can't believe it myself. I'll be goin' from Valdosta right to Daytona, my first National! And it's a short-track race, a quarter-mile clay track. I've raced more short-tracks than half-miles."

"Are you nervous?"

"Yeah, kind of. I raced some of the big guys last year. There are a number of Nationals around here between May and mid-July. In late May, Springfield, Illinois has a mile race, and in June and July, Louisville and Lima both have half-mile races. Then the riders head back west for the Oklahoma City National. While they're in the area, there are a number of semi-pro races, usually on the nights before the Nationals. Some real "hot shoes" show up because it's easy money. They're used to winning, so if a local unknown wins the race, or is in the winners' circle, it's a big deal."

"Did you surprise any of them last year?"

"I took second at the short-track event outside of Louisville. A National Number won it, but I had plenty of them right behind me, I mean right behind me, close enough to have their teeth sunk into my rear tire."

"So, this is it?"

"Yeah, it looks like the real thing."

"Then I guess I won't see you in school on Monday." The realization swept across her mental landscape like a winter blizzard blowing suddenly out of nowhere.

"I can pick you up after school if you want."

"If I want? You know that I want you to." God, it would be different without Billy in school.

"If the weather's nice, I'll pick you up on my bike. If it's cold, I'll try to borrow my mom's car. So, let's say I meet you in front of the school around 3:20. Okay?"

"Okay, and Billy…" She wavered some, not knowing if she should say it. "Look, Billy, I just want you to know, it might sound crazy…I'm sure my father would think so…but I just want you to know that I think you made the right decision."

"Thanks. I appreciate that."

"I'll see you tomorrow. Okay?"

"I'll be waitin' for you at 3:20 in front of the school. Good night, Praxy, and…sweet dreams."

"Yeah, sweet dreams to you too."

She set the receiver down softly, picked up her magazine and placed it on the nightstand, and then got up from her bed. Standing in the center of the room, she had a strong urge to pick the phone back up and telephone him. She reached down, grabbed the receiver, and held it tightly against her, feeling its hardness against her cotton nightgown. She wanted to tell him once more that she believed in him and in his dream and that she was, at the same time, even envious. Yes, envious! To have a dream like Billy's and not pursue it wouldn't be just sad, she reflected. It would be far worse. It would be tragic.

CHAPTER SIX

It's three in the friggin' morning. I still can't sleep. I woke up completely soaked, my T-shirt and shorts bathed in sweat and the sheets dripping wet. All I remember is an ear-shattering explosion, a bright flash, and a scream cutting through me like the ragged edge of a rusty fender. I buzzed for Stockton and asked him to bring me something, anything. He told me to calm down, that it was just a dream. Then I noticed how his expression changed from being pissed, for calling him in the middle of the night, to something else, maybe a kind of official concern. He asked me how I felt. I told him I wasn't doing so well, that I needed something to relax me. I'm sure he could see that. He said he couldn't give me any pills, not without getting permission from Phillips first. That would mean telephoning him, waking him up and all, since at this hour in the morning he would be asleep. I pleaded with him to give me something and promised I wouldn't say a word to Phillips. He insisted that he wasn't allowed to administer drugs without Phillips's okay, unless I wanted an aspirin. That he could give me.

Finally, I gave up. It was clear that he wasn't going to give in. I must have sounded like a fruitcake. The day before, I got into a big argument with him about not taking drugs, now I was begging like a junkie for a fix. After he left the room, I tried to go back to sleep. I scooted over to the edge of the bed, outside the sweaty trough my body had formed in its center.

This room gives me the creeps. It's as quiet as a morgue, except outside my door now and then when I hear the odd clicking of heels on the tile. Which is seldom. Real seldom.

Sometimes I wonder if this isn't all a horrible nightmare. Or maybe worse. Maybe I'm dead! That would explain a lot of things, in particular the morgue-like atmosphere of this place. Yeah, I'm dead, and I'm only dreaming I'm awake, only dreaming that I'm alive. Reminds me of a quote Mrs. Graystone put on the board once. It was from one of Shakespeare's plays. "We are such stuff as dreams are made on, and our little life is rounded in a sleep." At the beginning of class, she'd scratch out something on the board for us to write about in our journals. Usually the quotes didn't do much for me. I'm not what you'd call the literary type. And anyway some of them were really friggin' lame, like "Hitch your wagon to a star." I mean, what are you going to write about that? But this one, this thing about dreams, was different. Think about it! How can you prove that everything isn't some fantastic dream? Charlie once mentioned a book he read by Mark Twain. It was called *The Mysterious Traveler*, or *The Mysterious Stranger*. Something like that. Anyway it was about a guy who discovers that everything in the world, all the good, all the evil, everything that we love or loathe, all the wonderful things in life as well as all our sorrows and all our regrets, are nothing more than thoughts coming from one lonely mind. And whose mind is it? Mine! How pathetic! Wouldn't it be a mind-blower to discover that! That everything is "dream stuff?" And if we are "the stuff that dreams are made on," then does it really matter what's outside this friggin' door?

There's only one catch. If reality is a figment of my imagination, why would I people it with guys like Stockton and Phillips? That's what I'd like to know. I'd have to be really loony, and desperately lonely.

Yeah, Phillips. The old guy isn't on the square. And all his indirectness is starting to get under my skin. He tells me that in time I'll understand things, but we must take it slowly. Take it slowly? For how long?

Earlier today, I asked him if this place is some kind of jail. The door being locked all the time sure as hell doesn't suggest that it's a hospital. When I confronted him with this, he told me that I should think of it as a hospital. As a hospital? All I can say is if it's a hospital, it's a very strange one. It's more like a bird cage. I feel like Tweety bird, and Stockton is some blundering Sylvester.

And Phillips? What's his role? Keeper of the cage? And who keeps him? To me, Phillips is a weird bird. Whenever I have a session in his office, he has me sit in one of these cheap plastic chairs, the kind they have in high school cafeterias, while he leans back in his black leather swivel-round. I sit there with my knees crossed, looking over his bulky desk. The guy rarely says a goddamn thing. He just leans his fat ass back in his chair and listens with the patience of a priest hearing the confession of some convict on death row. And whenever

I do have something to say that he thinks is important, he writes it down on this yellow legal pad.

There's a large window directly behind his desk, and his swivel-round is positioned such that I always sit facing the window and the glaring sun. For this reason, I generally see only a silhouette of him, or of his abnormally large, bulbous head. A head that always seems to be rimmed by fire in the late afternoons. Reminds me of one of those space photographs of the sun, you know, the ones you see in science books of a huge black ball with a thin circumference of dancing, orangey, yellow light. This hairless sphere of a head rests on a pear-shaped body, not unlike Humpty Dumpty's. He's a real crack-up, except for his eyes. They really spook me. When I look into them, or try to look into them, I kind of freak. It's probably attributable to his glasses. His glasses are as thick as coke bottles and behind the lenses, his eyes look like two tiny brown walnuts.

It's hard to trust a person when you're uncomfortable looking into their eyes.

Or if the person doesn't have a sense of humor.

I asked him once where the couch was. He looked at me kind of puzzled. I said you know, the couch? The sofa? Freud always had one for his patients. He gave this fake chuckle. A couch would sure as hell beat the plastic chair he has me sit in. I know my can would sure appreciate it.

This afternoon I noticed for the first time these two light green patches on his office wall. They're about eighteen inches long and ten inches high. They're a shade of green lighter than the rest of the wall. Which is an institutional puke green. Right next to them are two diplomas in thin black frames. One is from the University of Richmond and the other, I think, is from Western Reserve University. Those two patches baffle me. Was something removed for my benefit? And another crazy thing. Whenever I'm permitted to leave my room and go out in the hall, no one's around. It reminds me of the inside of a school building in the dead of summer. I get the feeling that only Stockton and myself occupy the entire floor. Every now and then Stockton's buddy, whatever his name is, pops his head in my room. I think his name's Pete, or something like that. He's a real goofy looking character. As skinny as a famine victim, with dark smudges around his eyes that look like he tried to remove his eye shadow but wasn't too successful. And the tight pants he wears look more like white dance skins than pants. Maybe the high heels I hear clicking down the hall late at night are his. Who knows what he and Stockton are up to. Wouldn't surprise me one bit if Stockton's a closet queen and his macho act is just some phony disguise.

Today, or yesterday rather, something really weird happened. Spooky weird. It occurred right at the end of our little chat, or our session rather, or more precisely, at the end of my monologue, since I'm usually the only one talking. Anyway, I had just finished telling Phillips about Praxy and the incident in history class with Coach Wilkins and his orangutans. Phillips just sat behind his desk, sat there twiddling a black pen between his chubby fingers waiting for me to continue. He acted like I had been telling him an Agatha Christie mystery and left out the part where the murderer's discovered. Finally he goes and breaks the silence and asks me if I remembered what I had originally set out to talk about. I said sure. Charlie. How I met Charlie. So I needed to tell him about Praxy first, since I met Charlie through Praxy. I met Charlie that same day at lunch. Praxy introduced me to him in the cafeteria while we were standing in line to get our lunch. I remembered her getting all excited telling Charlie about what happened in Coach Wilkins's class.

So again today Phillips asked me to try to describe Charlie to him in more detail. I started telling him how Charlie likes poetry and book stuff. That's the first thing that came to mind. He's just the crazy opposite of me. I'm not what you would call the studious type. Math's all right. It's kind of easy for me. Not that I'm one of those math geniuses, but I do occasionally help Praxy and Charlie with their homework. Of, course if it hadn't been for Charlie walking me through Macbeth, I think Graystone would have given me a fat F instead of a cute little C. Nothing's wrong with a C, as I see it. I don't think grades mean doodley squat anyway. I told Phillips I know some of the dullest students, some of them no smarter than his desk, who get all A's and B's.

There's this guy named Paul Benton, for example. Benton's on the honor roll every grading period, yet he's about as bright, gives off as much light, as a headless matchstick. He's not just dull, he's friggin' obnoxious. I remember once in English when the class was discussing the *The Grapes of Wrath*, Charlie's all-time favorite book. Slack Jaw Benton had a lot to say about it, especially the ending where Rose of Sharon, Tom Joad's sister, has this baby that's born dead. Uncle John sends it floating down this muddy stream formed in the road by a week or so of unending rain. The Joad family hasn't had what you would call many sunny days since departing from Oklahoma. Grandpa dies, then Grandma. Connie, Rose of Sharon's worthless husband, deserts her, and Noah, Tom's older brother, decides to take a stroll down the Colorado River and is never heard from again. Oh, yeah, and then their friend, and sort of spiritual adviser, Jim Casy, is beaten to death. Anyway, after the baby is sent on its way, Rose of Sharon enters this barn to escape the downpour. Inside she sees a middle-aged man. He's over in the corner in the pale light, stretched out in the straw. He apparently hasn't eaten for days and is on the brink of starving to death. Rose of Sharon goes over to him and takes his grizzled chin in her hands. Then she guides his mouth to one of her milk-swollen breasts, trying to nurse him back to health.

This was just too much for St. Paul. The candidness of the scene must have shocked his Jehovah Witness nerve fibers. He told Mrs. Graystone that that particular scene just summed up how awful the novel really is. And proved that Steinbeck was a master craftsman at cheap pornography and smutty sensationalism. The novel's only purpose was to arouse our prurient interests and sell copies to those who were looking for a cheap thrill. Well, Charlie was steaming. I thought he would just float out of his seat, like one of these hot air balloons. He managed to pull himself together enough to tell Benton that if he really understood the novel, then maybe, just maybe, he would appreciate the ending.

Paul-boy went on blabbing that had John Steinbeck been a true Christian, then his purpose would have been to show the terrible influence that Jim Casy, the preacher-turned-atheist, had had on a once righteous, God-fearing family. Then the novel would make some sense, and would have a moral message too. That way we might learn something of value from it. The reader would fear characters like Casy by seeing how he had brainwashed the Joads with his communistic ideas. And then they would understand how God's punishment was taking Casy's life and Rose of Sharon's baby's life. That way the author wouldn't have needed a strip tease scene at the end to sell his novel. This last scene, if it shows anything, he said, turning in his seat and looking straight at Charlie, only shows to what depths of moral depravity poor Rose of Sharon's soul had sunk.

I told Phillips that Charlie was fit to be tied. His eyes were as large as the valves in a Harley XR 750— about the size of silver dollars, that is. He kept snapping the knuckles of his right hand while he stared at Benton. The class was stone silent, waiting for Charlie to say something. He shot a glance at Mrs. Graystone and then back at Paul. "You know something Benton," he said, "if you could ever just once slip out of that straightjacket of your religious brainwashing, you might see some real beauty where now you see only ugliness and sin. I feel sorry for you."

I about went friggin' nuts. Charlie has a way with words, and that was just pure and simple poetry coming out of him. I put my two fingers up to my lips and let loose a shrill, glass-shattering whistle. And then I clapped several times, as loud as I could. I thought I was the only one in the room brave or foolish enough to make such a big deal out of what Charlie had said. And then I heard this small, light clap, clap, clap from the other side of the room. It was Praxy. I remember looking at her and then at Charlie. We smiled boldly at each other like three compatriots who had just knocked down the Mighty Tower of Babel. Even Mrs. Graystone was busy fighting back a tiny smile forming in the corner of her mouth. Then after regaining her composure, she said in this pleasant school-teacher voice of hers that they had heard quite enough on *that* particular subject.

But that wasn't the end of it. Later, after class, right after we had left the room and were walking down the hall together to go to our other classes, here comes Benton and his Holy Rollin' sidekick, Cindy Chapley. She's another one of your dufus honor roll students. The two of them came strutting pompously over to us. She had on this dumpy dress, one of those real out of date fashions that looks like a Wallmart special that your grandmother wouldn't be caught dead in. Oh yeah, and she had this big silver cross dangling from her neck, the kind you see in the horror movies used to ward off vampires. Believe me, she didn't need the cross. Her face would have done the job. It has these freckles splattered all over it that make you think that maybe someone dipped a brush in a pile of loose cow manure and then flicked it at her. I mean, she's just totally revolting. Her lips are always formed into this disgusting pout that makes her look like she's squatting on the toilet trying to take a dump.

Anyway, like I was saying, the two of them come up to us, and right away Benton starts flapping his jaws again like some wild evangelist having a seizure. He tells Charlie that he might think he's cute now with his wisecracks about religion and straightjackets, but God wouldn't find it very amusing.

And then Cindy starts up. "You thought you were so cool in there, especially with your two atheist friends to support you." She was unconsciously holding her cross out in front of her, to protect her from us heathens.

"Look," Praxy said indignantly. She was full of it up to here. "Just because we're not fire and brimstone Baptists doesn't mean we don't believe in God. And even if we don't, it's no concern of yours." And then really sarcastically. "Anyway, I'm sure your God will see to it that we're punished for reading porno. Yes, he'll turn us over on his big fatherly knee, drop our drawers, and spank us right good, right on our naked butts. Yes, right on our *naked little butts.*"

"Yeah, just keeping joking, Praxy, because he who laughs last always laughs longest." I guess the reference to naked butts, especially coming from a girl, embarrassed him. I remember his zits turning a shade of deep purple.

"What an idiot," Praxy said. "Certainly an honor student should be able to come up with something just a little more original than 'He who laughs last always laughs longest.'"

I remember looking over at Benton and Cindy and then thinking, and they're honors students? What a waste. They'll both probably go off someday and join a fanatical religious cult and become mass murderers. Like the crazy Davidian bunch in Whacko, Texas.

When I had finished telling Phillips all this, he was quiet. He didn't say a word, just leaned back in his leather chair, folded his hands together, and rested them on his fat gut. I thought how strange it was that at no time had he found my story even slightly amusing. I mean, I thought it deserved at least an occasional snicker. Maybe he didn't care to hear me take a jab at religious fruitcakes. For all I knew, he was a Born Again Baptist.

"Is something wrong?" I asked. The truth is I felt good. If I had offended his religious sentiments, too bad. I find people like Paul and Cindy both dangerous and amusing. Real freaks. If he didn't like my sense of humor, then fine. He could lump it. I didn't care for holier than thou bastards anyway.

"No. It's just that I'm waiting to hear some more about Charlie."

His remark surprised me. What the hell did he mean? I had just finished telling him about Charlie. Had he been listening? Could he really be that obtuse?

"I just told you a lot about Charlie," I said.

"No, I mean I would like you to tell me what he looks like. You haven't said a thing about his looks. I was waiting for you to describe him. Is he cute? Tall? Well-built?"

Christ, what kind of question was that? Was Phillips serious? Did he get his kicks that way? What the hell, if that's what turned him on. "Well, he's a little shorter than me, and he has hair the color of, the color of… "

"Yes?"

Wow! This was unreal! Something really freaky was happening. I could tell him about Charlie, I mean I had just finished telling him about Charlie, how Charlie is and all, but when I tried to get a friggin' picture of Charlie in my mind, I couldn't. Each time I tried to see Charlie's face, there was nothing there. Well, not exactly nothing. It sends shivers through me right now just thinking about it. What I mean is I couldn't make out a face, only a shadowy outline of a face. Well, not exactly an outline either. This is going to sound too crazy…but all I was able to see was a freaky circle of light dancing in the outline where a face should be. Yeah, just this blinding light. It was the kind of image you see when someone shoots a camera flash directly in your eyes. A bright dancing ball of light.

Phillips encouraged me to continue. He wanted me to look closer. Even if it hurt. He thought it was important that I find some detail, any detail. He said if I wanted to get better, it was important that I see something.

I felt giddy again and didn't want to continue, yet he kept insisting that I shouldn't give up now. So, I tried again. But right when I thought I was about to see Charlie's face, right at that moment, another bright flash went off, this time even more blinding, more intense. More like an explosion than a flash. It was really crazy. I had to press my thumbs hard against my eyes to shut it out. Really hard. I waited until I could see only a watery red blur. It was the only way to erase the painful image. The only way, that and pushing Charlie out of my thoughts altogether.

I told Phillips I thought I was going to be sick and couldn't go on, that I felt exhausted and that I wanted to suspend for today. Suspend, that's one of his words. Sometimes he asks me if I would like to "suspend" our discussions until I feel more like talking. Some kind of medical jargon, I guess. Anyway I told him that tomorrow I would try again, that is if he thought I should. I wasn't so sure myself. Maybe it would be better to wait. I wasn't exactly keen on the idea. He thought that we were on the threshold of some discovery that I needed to make. He said it was only a matter of time now until I got better, that maybe after I had a good sleep, we could resume. He said we might have a go at it again in the morning, if I was up for it. I felt faint and my stomach was all knotted. I told him that I wanted to go back to my room and lie down. I asked him if he could give me something to relax me. He said sure. Then he wallowed out from behind his desk, and for the first time during the session, I could see him clearly. His glasses had slipped down and looked like they were about to slide off the tip of his nose. I looked behind his thick lenses. His eyes no longer appeared small and distorted. No, they were much larger than I imagined. Fanning out from his corneas were tiny red veins that intersected each other, like roads on a map, crisscrossing each other and stretching out over the thin white membrane of his eyeballs. His eyes looked as weary and worn out as I felt, and for a second, I felt sorry for him. Why? I guess I didn't really know. Maybe because he hadn't been able to help me. My loss was his loss.

He came up beside me, put his flabby arm over my shoulder, and walked me to the door. "Let's try again tomorrow," he said softly.

"Dr. Phillips," I said. I felt small next to him, though he isn't by any means a tall man, maybe an inch or two taller than me. "I'm not sure if I want to see Charlie right now, even if you brought him here. I know that sounds horrible, not wanting to see your best friend. It's just that…it's just that I don't think I'm ready to see him. I'm not even sure if I'd recognize him. Dr. Phillips, am I really whacko or what?"

"You just need to sort out a few things, that's all," he said earnestly. When you're ready Charlie will come to you. When that happens, you'll recognize him."

Now I wait till morning. Sleep. I need to think sleep, I tell myself, pulling the damp pillow against me. Tomorrow I'll see Phillips again. That is if I'm to confront this Charlie thing. For now, I just need to sleep.

CHAPTER SEVEN

Charlie floated around on Nike Air Jordons all week. This was the weekend of the National at Daytona, and his parents agreed he could join Billy there for Easter break, provided he promise to take his school work with him and be back home in time for dinner Sunday night and school Monday morning. Billy would pick him up at the Daytona Beach airport Thursday afternoon. He would only stay for four days. Friday night he would go with Billy and Chuck to a pro half-mile race, and then truck over to the stadium on Saturday for the first Grand National of the season. And Billy would be in it! Maybe even in the final! First he'd have to make it through the time trials and his qualifying heat. For Billy, the time trials wouldn't be a problem. The qualifying heats, now that would be different. The best racers in the entire country would be there, so Billy would have to do some impressive racing to make the final event.

Recently Charlie had been going down to Bradley's Harley Shop and hanging around while Billy and Chuck, Tom Bradley's shop mechanic, toyed on the dyno, tuning Billy's 600 c.c. Rotax. The weather had been great for late February, in the high 50's most of the week, so Charlie had his Honda out every day, and in the afternoon after school he'd cruise down to the shop. He'd been catching flak from the guys at the shop for riding a Japanese bike.

"Why don't yuh buy a real scooter, instead of that rice-paddy jumper!"

"Yeah, whaddaya ridin' that slant-eyed thing for anyway? Why don't yuh get a real machine? Trade that rice burner in for a Harley."

There was a Buy American Fever in the air, so riding around on a Japanese motorcycle or in a Japanese car was asking for it, especially from middle-class Americans who were experiencing the biggest economic downturn in decades. Some of them even went as far as to believe there was a national conspiracy on the part of Japan to get back at the U.S. for Nagasaki and Hiroshima. The Japanese revenge. Charlie thought he might have discovered the basis of this paranoia, after spending a semester with a foreign exchange student from Germany.

For several years now, McKinley High School had maintained an exchange program with schools in France and Germany. The program was sponsored by the high school German and French clubs. Because Charlie had taken German since eighth grade, he was a veteran member of the German club. In his sophomore year, his parents agreed to let one of the exchange students from Germany live with them for a semester.

Hans Gunther was friendly enough. But Charlie saw a side of him that reminded him of the guys at the shop. In his tenth grade class, they were studying world history, and when they got to The Second World War, the subject of ovens and Jews naturally came up. His history teacher showed them a film of the allies liberating one of the concentration camps in Poland. Charlie felt nauseous when he saw this huge pit filled with grisly, twisted corpses, yet he forced himself to sit through the film. Later that day in his German language class, while he was reading a passage on Bach, a scene from the movie seemed to rise from the page in front of him. As he looked down at the painting of Bach, he saw the anguish-torn faces of a dozen or more naked, emaciated Jews huddled together in a barren, concrete detainment room. His soul froze as they stared up at him with their sickly eyes and thin, bloodless lips. He pressed his knuckles tightly against his eyeballs, forcing himself to shut the image from his mind and return to the painting of Bach. Though he succeeded, one haunting thought remained. How could the German nation, a nation that produced Bach, Beethoven, and Goethe sit still and speechless and watch as Hitler sent off nearly six million human beings to the ovens to be gassed?

A couple of days after this incident, he went to the public library and checked out a novel called *Sophie's Choice.* He had heard about the movie. As he was reading the novel, he came upon this part where the author speculates about the kind of people Hitler relied on to help him with his "final solution." It had something to do with a special kind of bureaucratic mentality. These bureaucrats perceived of efficiency as their One True God. And when their minds were presented with the problem of getting rid of six million Jews, they set to work to solve the problem in the most efficient way. They fed them just enough to keep them going, until their replacements would arrive. And they worked them day in and day out like inhuman slaves. Then right at the time the boxcars unloaded the camp's new inmates, the former inmates, on the brink of collapse, were herded off to the gas chambers. Perfect timing. No people in the history of the world had ever devised such an ingenious plan. Since their aim was to exterminate a race of people, and not keep them as slaves, it was perfectly conceived.

Charlie and Hans were in the same history class. One night after dinner, when they were alone up in Charlie's room, Charlie got up the nerve to ask him what he thought of the Holocaust. Hans was silent for what seemed an interminably long time. Finally he turned to Charlie and said that he probably felt the same way that many Americans felt about Japan and the two atomic bombs they dropped.

Hans had a solution for dealing with any guilt he might feel forming on the horizon of his conscience. It was called pointing the finger. All he had to do was point it at others who had committed war atrocities. Though he never perceived this as a form of denial, that's what it was. Simple and pure denial. Not the act itself, Charlie realized. The atrocities had been committed. That was a matter of historical record. But the seriousness of the act, that was another thing. The way out was to find some other guy to blame. Then it would be just another one of those things that happens during wartime.

So whenever Charlie was teased about his Honda, he tried not to let it bother him because he suspected that at the bottom of it all, it wasn't just a matter of the Japs taking our jobs. It went much deeper than that. It had to do with shared guilt and denial.

Billy had called Charlie early in the morning and said he would drop by the school around 3:20 and pick up Praxy. He wanted to take advantage of the rare, unseasonably mild winter weather. Praxy loved going for bike rides, so this would be a real mid-winter treat.

Out in front of the school, the sun glowed timidly, emitting about as much warmth as an old cast iron radiator plugged with rust and age. It had begun to nestle into the deep indigo folds of sky spreading out from the horizon's edge. The three-story brick school building stretched its inky shadow across the concrete parking lot. Hoping to absorb the sun's last pallid rays, Charlie had parked his motorcycle just outside the building's sprawling shadow.

He stood half-leaning against his Honda, his brown aviation jacket unzipped to the waist. Cupping his hands to his mouth, he blew into them. Then he rubbed them together to generate a little heat. He cringed as he felt a small, cold hand on the back of his neck.

"Nice bike, dude. Think I can catch a ride?" Praxy laughed, her voice as light and musical as wind chimes.

"Christ, Prax. Your hand's like an ice cube."

Just then Charlie saw Billy swing around the corner on his Triumph Bonneville, a 70's model with a faded purple and white teardrop tank. In one smooth movement, he came to a stop in front of both of them, killed the engine, and toed the side stand out, leaning the bike over on its side. He'd bought the motorcycle from a truck driver whose friend had been killed returning from Cedar Park, an amusement park close to Lake Erie. It had been raining, and while attempting to overtake a truck, he had a head-on collision with an on-coming car. Nothing was left of him or the bike. After his friend's death, the truck driver decided to park the Triumph. When Billy asked the him how much he wanted for the bike, he said to just take it. Though the Triumph had sat for years, there were no visible signs of rust on it. The truck driver had sprayed it with W.D. 40. Underneath the thick layer of oil and years of accumulated dust, the bike was in near perfect shape, with only twelve thousand miles on it.

"Hi, Prax," Billy said, his ducks tails flattened back like he had just come out of a wind tunnel at an automatic car wash. The black leather jacket he always wore was zipped up tightly around his neck. "Man, the weather's friggin' beautiful. Can't believe it's February."

"Yeah, beautiful weather," Praxy echoed. She had on a pair of black slacks, and over them a knee-length, red wool coat with brass buttons. She reached up and adjusted a silver braid that kept her hair tied back. A couple of unwieldy curls had popped loose. "When you guys are in Florida, I'm the one who'll be catchin' all the rays," she said, smoothing down her curls. "Looks like all the sunny weather's come north. I heard on TV last night that northern Florida has a frost alert in effect. You guys will probably come back from Daytona as white as sheets."

"Don't count on it, Praxy," Charlie said. "More likely we'll be layin' on the beach checkin' out the gals passing by in string bikinis. And thinkin' about you back home curled up next to the fireplace tryin' to thaw out your pinkies."

"My what?"

"Your pinkies. Your toes. What did you think I meant?"

"You confused her when you said something about girls in string bikinis," Billy laughed.

Praxy shook her head sideways in mock disapproval, smiling at them as though they were two naughty boys too ingenuous to deserve a larger reprimand.

"Hey, did you get the Rotax all tuned and ready?" Charlie asked, judiciously changing the topic.

"Yeah. We put it on the dyno this morning. The baby's crankin' out about sixty-eight horse. I don't think Parker gets that much out of his, and Harley-Davidson's tunin' up his friggin' bikes for him."

"Harley-Davidson?" Praxy asked.

"Yeah, Scott Parker and Chris Carr are Harley-Davidson sponsored riders. After a race, Harley goes over their bikes completely. Their mechanics don't replace rings, they put in new pistons. You know, it pisses a lot of guys off, privateers, those who own their own bikes or are sponsored by local shops. Personally, I try not to let it bother me. Factory riders lose races too. They're not unbeatable. Anyway, I can't think about it. If I do, my mind's not on what it should be on—the race. And to be fair about it, Harley-Davidson doesn't win races for them. They win races for Harley-Davidson."

"How many other motorcycle companies sponsor riders?" Praxy asked.

"Dirt Track?"

"Yeah."

"Other than Harley-Davidson, only Honda, but they aren't really fully into Dirt Track racing. Lately though, their bikes have won some races. If this keeps up, who knows, maybe they'll get into it more. I'd ride for them, if they asked me, which isn't very likely."

"Wouldn't you rather be 'true and blue' and ride a Harley?" Charlie asked, playing with the visor on his helmet, unconsciously sliding it up and down.

"I'm not into flag waving. A Honda factory ride would do fine. I know the guys at work kid you about your Honda. I'm not sure they mean all that much. They're just repeatin' things they hear. Honda makes a good product. I ride this old Triumph," Billy said, rapping lightly on the tank, "not because I care about what the guys at work say, but because I like old British bikes. Hell, if I had the money, I would pick up an old Norton Commando, one of those black ones with gold pin stripes."

Charlie felt a little embarrassed. It was stupid of him, he thought, to imagine Billy in the same class as the guys at the shop. "You and Chuck have much more to do on the Rotax?"

"No. Chuck just wanted to pull the head and flow it. That shouldn't take too long though."

"Well, I finished my work in study hall today, except history, and that won't take me more than five minutes. I got some free time, if you don't mind me tagging along again."

"Hey, no problem. After we take Prax home, you can cruise down to the shop with me. While Chuck has the head off, I need to change the air filter and the rear shocks."

"Great. Maybe I'll fool with my Honda while you're working on the Rotax. I could gap the plugs and blow out the air filter."

"Sure, why not. Maybe you'll pick up some other tips on bike maintenance." Then turning to Praxy, "You're welcome to join us, Prax."

"Sorry, guys. Doesn't sound all that interesting. Anyway, I have some serious math homework."

"What do you say about this? After you're done with your homework, say about seven, we all meet at my house to celebrate?"

"Celebrate?" Praxy asked, her soft brown eyes dispelling the darkening tones of late afternoon. "Celebrate what? Do you have any idea what he's talking about?" she said, smiling teasingly at Charlie.

"No. Can't say I do," Charlie beamed, his upper lip rolled back, showing his pearly whites. "Bradley give you a raise?"

"I'm a friggin' Expert now! Come on, guys, like you didn't know. What do you think Daytona's all about?"

"Oh yeah, Daytona. I almost forgot," Charlie said, trying to keep the game alive.

"Look, Mom won't be home. She's workin' night shift. I'll pick up drinks and chips."

"Sounds fine," Praxy said. "I'll think up something to get out of the house early. We should be done with dinner by six or six-thirty."

"Well, in that case, we better scoot if I'm goin' to give Chuck a hand with the bike. Hop on, Prax," Billy said, reaching behind him and patting the smooth leather seat. He slid a helmet off the handlebar mirror. Whenever he took Praxy for a ride, he brought along an old, scuffed up helmet. It was one of those early sixties models without a chin guard. He'd bought it at a garage sell for five dollars.

"Here, Prax, your lid," he said, taking the helmet by the strap and tossing it to her.

She reached out and caught the helmet, pulling it into her chest like a football. "No thanks, I'm fine," she smiled, pitching it back to him. She gracefully swung a leg over the rear fender and plopped down on the seat behind Billy.

"You sure?"

She put her arms around his waist. "I always feel boxed in with that stupid thing on my head."

Charlie had already put on his helmet and was fumbling with the strap, trying to fasten it. It was a black full-coverage Bates with a racing stripe down the middle. "Come on, now. I'm not going to be the only one with a helmet on, am I?" he said, sounding a note of chagrin.

"Whoso would be a man must be a nonconformist," Praxy teased.

"Whoso would save his ass must wear a helmet," Charlie quipped back.

"Only if that's where you wear yours," Praxy joked. She looked so sexy. The legs of her black slacks had slid up, revealing her shapely calves.

"Billy, talk some sense into the girl," Charlie said helplessly. How stupid he felt. Billy rarely if ever wore a helmet, and now he was asking him to convince Praxy to wear one.

Billy swung his head around and looked over his shoulder and smiled at Praxy. He said nothing. It was Praxy's decision.

"Come on, Praxy, don't be stubborn. What do you have to prove anyway?" Charlie said, raising his voice. I don't want to make a big deal out of it. But why do you think that most states have helmet laws? I mean, they're just like seatbelt laws."

"Laws to protect you from yourself. Sounds like a contradiction to me. Is that the kind of society you want?" Billy retorted.

"Doesn't the government have to play Big Brother sometimes? For our own good? Or are you for repealing safety belt laws too?"

"Come on, Charlie, you aren't serious?" she laughed.

"But I am."

"Hey, look, Charlie, why don't you two continue this debate when I'm some other place? Before we go down to the shop, I'd like to pick up a primary cover gasket for my bike. It's starting to drip a little oil. Maybe we can stop by Pop Reymand's." Billy bent over the side of the bike and began tickling the carburetors, pushing the small priming buttons on the top of each carburetor up and down several times. Charlie could smell the gas flooding the carbs.

"Look, Billy, I don't want to, what do they say, 'beat a dead horse,' but really, man, don't you think certain laws are for our own good? I know wearing a helmet in this state isn't a law, but if it was a law, wouldn't it be for our own good?"

Billy leaned over the front of the bike and wiped the gasoline from his fingers onto the front tire. "Charlie, the real reason we have to wear helmets is to save money, not lives. You don't really think the government gives a good whiz, do you? It's the insurance companies, man. The insurance companies care about saving millions of dollars from liability claims. It's dollars, man. Not lives. Hospital stays are expensive, and the insurance companies realize that when they pick up the check. Now, if you really want to know how I feel, here it is. Nobody, in my opinion, not the mayor, the governor, the president, the pope, or even Sting," Billy knew how crazy Charlie was about Sting, "no one has any business telling you how to live your life. It's your life, man, not anyone else's. Okay?"

Charlie gave his helmet strap a frustrated yank and felt it tighten against his chin. Then his eyes met Praxy's. "Sure, whatever you say. It's your head, not mine."

"God, Charlie, thanks for giving us our heads back," Praxy said.

On the way to Praxy's house, Billy and Charlie took the main boulevard that cut through the southwest corner of town. Charlie glanced at the elongated shadow of himself and his motorcycle floating out in front of him in the paling light. It streamed over the pavement, encountered a car, and then glided over its smooth contours. He listened to the steady hum and light valve clatter of his twin-cylinder engine. A few minutes before, in front of the school, the weather had been mild, spring-like, but now, clipping along at forty miles per hour, the cold air began to numb his fingertips and the tip of his nose. He lowered his left hand to a few inches above the left cylinder. The warm air that wafted upward from the engine soothed the cold tingling in his fingers.

Up ahead Praxy's red coattails flapped wildly against the sides of Billy's Triumph like the wings of a giant cardinal pumping up and down frantically against a forty mile-per-hour headwind. Charlie watched her withdraw a hand from Billy's jacket pocket and fumble with her silver braid. She turned around, waved and smiled. God, how cute she was. Billy was one lucky guy. For a few seconds he imagined Praxy on the back of his bike, her arms squeezed tightly around him, her soft, warm breasts pressed firmly against his back.

The steady, pulsating hum of the engine underneath him had an exhilarating effect on him. He leaned his bike slightly left, then right, swaying with its fullness, feeling its vibrating weight against the inside of his thighs. He squeezed his knees against the side of the tank, pressing against its satiny smoothness and its gentle curves. As he rolled back the throttle, the bike bucked and shot forward. His legs tightened on the tank and his blood surged as he felt the throb of the motor through the handlebars and seat. As he whipped by Billy, he saw the red blur of Praxy's coattail at the same time he felt it smack against the side of his tank.

Once in front of them, he let the throttle snap shut and felt the bike's inertia drag him back from wherever he had been.

Billy shot up next to him. "Christ, man, what are you tryin' to do? You almost took us out," he screamed, his voice barely audible above the rumble of his motor. He wasn't mad, just surprised at Charlie's carelessness.

"Maybe I'd better strap on a helmet," Praxy yelled out and then smiled her sexy smile.

"Sorry," Charlie shouted back. God, she was lovely. He thought about her hands in Billy's jacket pocket. Once in study hall he watched her writing in her notebook, and at the time he felt like reaching over and touching the back of her smooth, white hand.

Billy slowed to make a right turn. His bike backfired and a bluish-gray plume of smoke shot from his right tailpipe. They were entering the Heights.

Charlie often wondered what Billy thought about the glamour of the Heights, about the red brick streets lined with imposing mansions on either side, the sprawling lawns and neatly trimmed hedges, the flower gardens, the Mercedes and BMWs, the quiet, dreamlike orderliness of the place where peace and prosperity seemed to scent the air. There were times when even Charlie thought that the Heights was too unreal. He asked Praxy once why the Collie dog next door never barked. It acted like it wanted to. It threw its head back and snapped silently at the air, but never gave out the smallest yip. She told him that it had been operated on, which meant its vocal cords had been slit. The price of peace— castrated, barkless dogs.

As they came to a stop in front of her house, one of the two brick-faced Colonials on the street, Praxy quickly dismounted and then kissed Billy on the cheek. "See you guys later!" She ran off toward the house, then stopped suddenly and turned to Charlie and yelled out, razzing him one last time. "Keep that lid on. The life you save may be your own."

Charlie could feel his face burning. He wanted to reply with something witty, or funny. Anything! But she was gone. Why had he brought up the helmet business anyway? Now every time she had the opportunity to tease him about wearing a helmet, she would.

Billy revved his bike twice. It backfired and then cleared out, its deep explosions resonating through the neighborhood.

"Damn! Billy, you'll have the cops here!" What was he doing? Trying to make some statement? Piss off the Heights people? Now that's all Charlie needed, for his father to hear that he was tearing through the Heights on his motorcycle. His father worried enough as it was about Charlie and the bike. And his mother. His mother had tried to talk him out of buying a motorcycle. She had this idea that guys who rode them were these unwholesome types, guys with star-studded leather jackets and cigarettes dangling from their lower lips. His father had been mildly opposed to the idea of his only son owning a motorcycle, but since it was Charlie's own money, money he had saved over the summer working as a clerk at the local pharmacy, he gave in and agreed to let him buy the Honda.

"The plug in the right cylinder is fouling out. I just thought I'd clean it out, burn the oil."

So he hadn't wanted to prove anything or make any statement. Charlie looked down at his helmet. Shit! How

Billy made him feel like an ass! He seemed to be always misjudging Billy's intentions. He fumbled with its strap. All the warmth had gone out of his fingertips. They felt clumsy and numb as he tried to fasten the strap under his chin. "Yeah," he mumbled, "I was going to tell you that I noticed your tailpipe blow out a cloud of smoke when you turned off the boulevard." Pissed at himself, he gave the starter button a brutal push and the engine caught.

"I want to stop by Pop Reymand's before we go to the shop."

"I'll follow you," Charlie said. He jerked the zipper of his jacket up tightly against his chin. A shiver traveled down his arms as he watched Billy pull away into the gray dusk. As he listened to the rumbling staccato of Billy's low-slung mufflers echoing through the Heights, he told himself next time he would reserve judgment. He'd give Billy the benefit of the doubt before he pronounced him guilty.

CHAPTER EIGHT

I don't feel like I slept much last night, but that's nothing new. How could any sane person sleep in a hole like this? Phillips says I should think of this place as a kind of hospital. Well, it doesn't look like a hospital. Or smell like a hospital. If it's a hospital, where's the staff? The nurses? The doctors? The other patients? And why can't I leave this ward, this part of the building? Wouldn't a nice little stroll around the grounds do me some good? A little fresh air? After all, it's a big place. I can see that much from my window.

Early this morning a black guy was out back with a lawnmower, the kind you ride on, an old green-and-white thing with a loud muffler. The grass, what there is of it, wasn't high at all, just full of Queen Anne's lace. It seems the black guy cuts the grass about once every two weeks. But I never see anybody water it. That's why it's so brown. Guess they want to keep it from growing. Apparently the place is understaffed. The guy on the mower is the only person I've seen, that is outside of Phillips, Stockton, and Stockton's pal Pete.

Phillips came for me right after breakfast, if you can call it that—two pieces of burnt toast, a hardboiled egg, a paper cup with two medicine tablets, and a tiny glass of grapefruit juice. Absolutely sumptuous. We went to his office, and I plopped down again in the hard plastic chair. I wouldn't doubt that the Marquis de Sade holds a patent on them. Phillips leaned back in his swivel-round and peered over his thick glasses. He wanted to know if I felt like trying to remember some things me and Charlie had done together. He said to forget about Charlie's face for now and start by remembering places we used to go together. He said I should try to recall the places as vividly as I could.

I'm not sure why, but Pop Reymand's came to mind. I was thinking about the time Charlie and I went to Pop's. I used to go there if I needed anything for my Triumph. I have an old Bonneville that I bought about two years ago. I love the friggin' thing. It has a deep, throaty sound to it, not the tinny sound of a Japanese bike. It's also a rare machine.

I told Phillips that I was supposed to meet Charlie and Praxy after school. My plan was to swing by the school and pick Praxy up and then take her home. After dropping her off, I'd head over to Pop's with Charlie. I remember it was cool but unseasonably warm for February.

The Heights is the classy side of town. We plebeians live across the highway in the Dumps. That's an appropriate name for it. Praxy lives in this big house, looks kind of like Monticello. It has a funky statue of a black lantern boy out front, looks like one of Jefferson's escapees. He's dressed in a red jacket with white pants and a small red cap, the kind of cap racehorse jockeys wear. Charlie once made a comment about the lantern. He said it reminded him of this guy called Diogenes. He was an ancient Greek philosopher. Charlie said he slept in an urn at night and during the day went about with a lantern looking for an honest man. I told him if that's what the black lantern boy was doing over here in the Heights, he was likely to come up empty. Charlie asked me what I thought of the Heights. I told him nothing. Which is true. The place is too fairytale-like to be taken seriously. People don't live there. They withdraw there. It's about as lively as a Benedictine monastery. The only difference is the Heights is a bit flashier, and they bow down to a different god, called The Almighty Dollar.

I explained to Phillips that if the Heights were an appropriate name for Praxy's neighborhood, then the lowlands was a suitable name for mine. Or maybe, the trough. It has the right sound to it. You don't see Cadillacs parked out front, not new ones anyway. This black guy down the street does have an old, pink Cadillac Seville. But he's got it up on blocks. Our neighborhood's your typical working-class neighborhood, though there ain't many guys workin' these days. The people that live to the right of us, who share the duplex, are your typical trough dwellers. The woman's name is Agnes something-or-other, and her husband or boyfriend, or whatever he is, is named Mike. Lately, I haven't seen him at all. My mother told me he's in jail for beating up on her. Makes sense. They're always yelling and fighting, and the last time I saw her she had a big shiner. She looked like a friggin' raccoon. Come to think of it, she acts like one too. Kind of holes up inside. Usually I don't see her come out of the house except to check the mail. She's a skinny thing, never wears any makeup. Whenever I see her, she has on her bathrobe. It's one of those Walmart terry-cloth things that the colors fade out of a week after

91

you buy it. I doubt she ever gets dressed before one or two in the afternoon. I don't ever recall seeing her in anything but her ratty bathrobe.

Her husband, or this guy she lives with, is a painter. Not an artist painter, but a house painter. And like most painters I know, he's always tanked up. Of course, telling you that painters drink a lot is about the same as telling you that male dogs lift their legs when they take a whiz. Most evenings he's totally bombed out of his head, reeking of paint thinner and beer or cheap wine. His skin is the color of Georgia clay, from boozing and being outside all day. Outside, that is, until about five o'clock when all the bars open. He has deep wrinkles fanning out from the corners of his light blue eyes, like the prongs on a leaf rake. He probably gets the wrinkles from squinting into the sun, that is, when he's sober enough to work. I think he works for himself, pickin' up odd jobs here and there. When he finishes a job, he disappears for a couple of weeks, leaving Agnes to fend for herself. I think she's used to that because it looks like she's livin' on welfare. I saw her countin' out food stamps at the market once.

Phillips interrupted me, which he rarely does, and asked me if any of this had to do with Charlie, or with Charlie going to Pop Reymand's with me. I told him that I guess I got off the subject. Sometimes I do that.

Since my house wasn't too far from Pop Reymand's, I thought I'd stop by my house first and try to find the gasket I needed for my Triumph. I went down into the basement where I keep a bunch of junk parts. I remember looking quickly through some boxes in the fruit cellar. The damn place has cobwebs all over it. I had to pull them out of my hair. I had no luck finding the part. It was late in the afternoon, and I wanted to get down to Bradley's to do some last-minute prep on the Rotax, so Charlie and I left my house right away and headed for Pop's.

Pop Reymand's house is about a mile from my house. It's a one-story bungalow sided with cheap imitation brick, an asbestos-type material called Insulbrick. In the back of his house, he has a large four-car garage. This is where Pop lives. Hasn't spent a night in the house since his wife died, and that was well over ten years ago.

We pulled into the gravel driveway and parked our bikes close to the side entrance of the garage. The sun had nearly set, and the air was starting to get biting cold. I rapped on the side door and waited. No one came, so I rapped once again. I remember telling Charlie that Pop must be snoozin'. Every time I came over, he was takin' a friggin' nap.

We waited a minute or so, and then I heard this, "Okay, okay, I'm comin,'" and the slow, scraping shuffle of his shoes against the concrete floor. Then Pop's tired old face appeared in the window of the door. He must have fumbled with the lock for a full minute. Finally he pushed the door open and stood looking at us, his full head of stiff white hair sticking out in all directions. It looked like he hadn't run a comb through it in years. As usual, he was dressed in a blue workingman's uniform with grease stains up and down the front. I noticed that the fly to his pants was open. I didn't know if it was a matter of his memory giving out or if he just wasn't able to zip the thing up anymore, or didn't care to. Judging by the thickness of his glasses, he'd probably have difficulty finding his zipper.

Pop must be nearly eighty. Though his memory shows signs of wear and tear, a part of it is still vividly intact. He knows every greasy inch of his shop and every gritty bike part in it. And this is impressive, that is if you saw his shop. I tried to give Phillips an idea. I told him to imagine thousands of parts from nearly every British motorcycle ever made, strewn from one end of the garage to the other. It's like some guy backed a ten-ton dump truck into the garage, pulled the dump lever, and let the stuff tumble out onto his garage floor. Pop has mountains of tangled old parts stacked in heaps nearly to the ceiling. Remnants of Norton Commandos, Triumph Bonnevilles, Thunderbirds, Tiger Cubs, TR-6s, BSAs. Lightning Bolts and Victors, Royal Enfields, single cylinder AJSs and Matchlesses—and other bikes that disappeared from the scene only God knows when.

In the left rear of the garage is a pile of faded, rusty fenders thrown on top of each other in one twisted heap. Above the fenders, hanging from the rafters like coiled snakes, are tires. All kinds of tires. Knobby tires. Slick, bald, threadbare tires, as thin and as worn as the skin on the back of Pop Reymand's liver-spotted hands. In the middle of the garage, Pop has erected an amorphous mound of crankshafts, handlebars, foot pegs, clutch and brake cables, heads, cylinders, gas tanks, broken-down leather seats, and who knows what else. A workbench stretches along the right wall. It's spewing over with cardboard boxes, their sides bursting with yet more

94

greasy parts. And above the oil-stained workbench, gaskets hang from nails he's hammered into the cinder-block walls. All sizes of gaskets. Gaskets for engine cases, cylinders, transmissions. Even tiny carburetor gaskets!

His living area is in the center rear of the garage. It consists of an old gas furnace, a walled-in commode, a porcelain sink with permanent grease stains, an old round-cornered refrigerator, a foldup bed, a purple sofa with a few broken springs, a 24-inch black-and-white TV, a brown rectangular sofa table, a pile of magazines, a pile of dirty clothes, and his dog, Rufus.

Rufus is an old, gray, mangy-looking bloodhound that does nothing but sleep all day. He must be more than fifteen years old. I think he's comatose half the time. He never barks or goes to the door when someone knocks, but remains curled up in a deep sleep on this army blanket right next to the sofa. The blanket smells like urine. Maybe his bladder has gone out. If you go up to him and he's conscious, which is rarely the case, he just looks up at you with these red, droopy hound-dog eyes. He never moves his head, not even a bit, just keeps it plopped down on the floor. The loose skin hanging down from his upper jaw spreads out over the floor like a wet mop. When you move, his tired old eyes follow you around like radar, but his wrinkled head, which is as big as Pop's, just stays glued to the floor.

When we entered the garage with Pop, he flicked a light switch on beside the door and then asked us what we wanted. I said I needed a part for my bike.

"What is it yuh have?" he croaked, rubbing his stomach. Though he's as skinny as a clutch cable, he has this potato sack of a gut that spills over his belt.

"A 1974 Bonneville 650."

"Can't be a 650," he said.

Every time I go to his shop, he tells me the same thing.

"It's a '74 Bonneville 650 that was brought over from England or Europe," I explain to him. "I don't believe they ever sold any of them over here."

"Yeah, ain't many of "im around. Only seen a few of "im."

The few of them he has seen are probably all mine.

"They're the same as the 750. Only the cylinders and heads is different. So whadayuh need?"

I told him. And without even looking around the friggin' place, he said he couldn't help me.

"Are you sure? Maybe you got one layin' around somewhere," I said hopefully, nodding in the direction of the workbench.

"Look, I know what I have in here and what I don't have. Might not appear that way to yuh, but I know where things is. I'm tellin' yuh I don't have what yuh need. Why don't yuh try Warton's? Maybe he can help yuh."

"Pop," I said, trying not to laugh, "Warton's has been closed for at least five or six years."

"Yeah, well, I don't have what yuh want, so I can't help yuh. If you'll excuse me, I got some things I gotta take care of." He turned around and shuffled over toward the sofa, where Rufus was sprawled out sleeping on the dirty army blanket. "I ain't fed 'im yet, and it must be gettin' on noon."

It was actually about five in the afternoon, but I didn't see any point in telling him. What would it matter anyway? Noon? Five o'clock? It's not like he had a hot date planned.

"Don't look too hungry," he says, scraping some dog food out of a can into a red plastic bowl next to where Rufus lay. "But I know he is, 'cept he don't eat like he used tuh. 'Course, he don't do lots of things like he used tuh. Neither do I," he laughed hoarsely. "Seemed to 'ave lost his sense of smell. His kind make damn good huntin' dogs. Them type of dogs can smell a rabbit ten mile away."

"When was the last time you took him huntin'?" I asked, seeing that Pop was interested in talking about his dog.

"Never did. Don't like huntin'. Nor guns. Don't even eat meat no more. Not since my wife passed away." He walked over to the sink and grabbed a saucepan from a pile of unwashed dishes. Then he opened the refrigerator and took out a carton of milk. "Now she liked a big juicy steak and a baked potato. Could eat more red meat than a Saint Bernard. She was one of them big women. Now, Rufus here, he's got to have his meat. Tried gettin' him to stop eatin' meat once. Fed him rice and beans for a couple of weeks, and then one day I was foolin' around doin' a valve job on a motor, turned around, and he was plumb gone."

"Well, he obviously came back," I said.

"He came back all right. But he had me searchin' all around town for 'im. Even went down to the dog pound lookin' for 'im. Was afraid the dog catcher got 'im. Then about two days after he disappeared, he comes in the garage here, waggin' his tail like nothin' happened."

"So what did you do?"

"What'd I do? Fed him beans and rice for another couple uh weeks. And then one evenin', he hightailed it again."

"Yeah?" I said. "Then what?"

"This time I didn't go around lookin' for him. Figured he'd come home when he was good and ready, and lookin' for him was a waste of time. Well, he turned up about four days later. But not alone. He had this here rabbit clamped in his big ole jaw. Or what was left of a rabbit. It didn't have no head. He had chewed the damn head right off."

Pop started laughing about the missing head. He laughed so hard he had a coughing fit and turned all red and started choking. I patted him on the back a couple of times, and that seemed to take care of it.

"Well, that was it for the beans and rice," he said. "Dogs just wasn't meant to be vegetarians." He pushed the bowl of dog food closer to Rufus's nose. Rufus raised his head, sniffed the bowl, and then let his head sink down on the floor again. As he breathed in and out, the loose, baggy skin covering his jaws puffed up like a small balloon each time he exhaled. His breathing was slow and rattly.

"He doesn't look like he's too hungry," I said.

Pop didn't say anything for a while. He just looked at Rufus lying there on the frayed army blanket.

"He'll eat later. Look, I got some things to do. I can't help yuh with that part. Stop by Warton's. He'll probably have what yuh want. Like I said, I can't help yuh. Got things to do."

I remember as we left, Charlie asked me about Pop, how long he'd lived by himself, how long he'd had the shop, and so forth. He asked me if Pop had ever raced. I knew he had. Bradley had told me Pop was pretty damn good, became a National Number, even won a few important races. I told Charlie that Pop had once worked for Old Man Warton. At that time Warton had owned one of the largest British bike shops in northeastern Ohio.

Charlie wanted to know more about the old man's racing days. Everything I knew about Pop came from Bradley. I remembered Bradley saying that Old Man Warton had sponsored Pop. I imagine it wasn't cheap to get from one race to the next back then. It's not cheap today. And the distances between pro races that pay well is often hundreds of miles. You load up your equipment and head out, and if you don't make the final, or the top three spots in the final, you have a tough time coming up with enough cash to get to the next race, or even back home. At least that's how it is today, and I guess it was the same in Pop's day. Not a great way to...

I suddenly didn't want to continue with my story about Pop. Phillips was surprised. He wanted to know if it had anything to do with Charlie. I told him I wasn't sure. Maybe it did. He asked me how Charlie acted when I told him about Pop's racing days.

Then it struck me! I was on the brink of some discovery. About Charlie. And about me. I remembered Charlie asking me if I had any fears or doubts about my future. At first I wasn't real sure what he meant, what any of this had to do with what I was telling him about Pop.

"I'm not sure what you mean?" I said.

"Say things don't work out like you plan them."

"Do they ever?"

"Yeah, kind of. I guess it depends on your plans. Maybe you want to be a doctor, but you have trouble passing chemistry. Something like that. And then things get all fouled up."

"Well, I'm not plannin' to be any doctor. I don't like chemistry or biology all that much. I guess your plans have to be realistic. Is that what you're gettin' at?"

"Well, yeah, I guess. But even if they're realistic, things happen. Things like…"

"Like happened to Pop Reymand?" I said.

"Well, yeah, things like that," Charlie said tentatively, unsure of himself.

So that was it. Charlie wanted to know if I thought my life could end up like Pop's? I remember his remark really getting to me. What was wrong with Pop's life? He wasn't famous or anything. He wasn't any Cal Rayborn or Kenny Roberts or Scott Parker. He wasn't in any record books. Did that mean he was some kind of a failure? He had pretty much lived his life the way he wanted. It was doubtful that he had any real big regrets. None bigger than anyone else. Sure his life had had its ups and downs. Its disappointments. But that was true for everyone. Yet his life had been full. Fuller than most people's lives were. And Charlie was incapable of seeing this! He wanted to judge Pop by standards that didn't apply. And no outsider had a right to judge him. And Charlie was an outsider. Who was he to sum up anyone's life, for that matter? Mine or Pop's.

"And you think I might end up like Pop?" I came right out with it.

"No, of course not. Whatever gave you that idea? It's just that I feel sorry for the old guy. You know, livin' out back in a garage by himself, no one to look after him."

"Well, don't feel sorry for him. You don't have that right," I said coldly.

I saw how my words cut right through Charlie, but he deserved it.

I told Phillips that was probably the first time I saw the real difference between me and Charlie. Charlie couldn't avoid forming narrow views of others, others not like him. And for this reason, I knew we could never really be friends. Not close friends. The truth is he had let himself down more than he had me. He didn't want to understand people. He wanted to judge them. I remember, right after leaving Pop's, having second thoughts about Charlie coming down to Daytona with me and Chuck.

Phillips wanted to know if this was the only time I felt that way about Charlie. He wanted to know if we had ever quarreled about anything after this, if there were other times that I had been angry at him, wanted to get back at him, to punish him, to hurt him in any way.

At first I thought the questions were really off the friggin' wall. What was Phillips getting at? This creepy feeling came over me again that Phillips was hiding something, and that helping me was a secondary concern. It was then that I realized Charlie was the key to everything, and that Phillips was only interested in my stories if they had some connection with Charlie. I recalled that not once had Phillips mentioned anything about my parents, only that my mother had come by to see me. He said nothing when I told him I didn't recall the visit. Now is that normal? My mother comes by to see me, I don't recall anything about her being here, and Phillips doesn't act the least bit surprised.

If I could just remember more. There must be some way to dispel the fog.

Phillips is on to something. I can't deny that. And that something has to do with Charlie. Phillips knew that wasn't the only time Charlie had let me down. There was some larger thing that happened later. Sometime after Daytona. How long after I don't know, but I know it was sometime after I took off with Chuck for the West Coast and the national circuit.

Phillips wanted to know why I was silent. Then he said that if I couldn't remember any other times when I was upset with Charlie, that was okay. He asked me if I would like to suspend for now. If I felt like continuing later in the afternoon, I could buzz him. I agreed that would be best.

Before, I had told Phillips that if I could see Charlie once more and talk to him, Charlie could straighten things out. But I didn't insist on it. There's a part of me that is afraid to see him. I remember Phillips reassuring me, telling me it was only a temporary thing, that I would see Charlie when I was ready. Well, now I don't think I'll ever be ready. And maybe it's better that way. By blotting him out of my memory, I remove him from my life. I think that is easier. With him out of my life, I can go on. Yes! Blot him out! Forget him! Why dredge him up? Why not leave him at the bottom of the river?

Why?

Because by keeping him there, I know I'm burying a part of myself with him.

If I'm ever going to recover, I must face whatever there is out there to face. Phillips knows this. Today he helped me see something about Charlie I needed to see. Maybe tomorrow he will get me to see more.

According to old pecker hands, it's nearly nine o'clock. I decided to wait until tomorrow to see Phillips. Stockton should be coming by anytime with my fix. He's probably still pissed at me because I asked him, when he came to pick up my supper tray, why a big guy like him wanted to be a nurse. He said he wasn't a nurse. "What are you then?" I asked. He acted like it was a trick question. Which it was. I said, "If you're not a nurse or a doctor, then why the white outfit? Bakers, lab technicians, chemists, and medical people dress in white. So if you're not a nurse, then my next best guess would be you're a baker. How about baking me a nice, big chocolate cake? Chocolate's my favorite." He just glared at me and then snatched the tray from my bed. I thought the plates and stuff were going to fly off the tray. The guy can't take a joke.

So now I wait. A couple of pills and then beddy-bye. And tomorrow? Maybe I'll wake up and get lucky. And this whole pathetic nightmare will be over. I'll be back in Kansas and find out that Stockton wasn't the Wicked Witch of the West, just a guy who scoops ice cream for a living at some fancy restaurant in the Heights. That will explain his outfit.

CHAPTER NINE

Praxy informed her mother that she was going over to Liz Gradel's house after dinner to work on her math. She and Praxy had been friends since junior high school. Liz had this passion for collecting insects, dead insects, that is, mostly wasps and bees. Hanging on the four walls of her bedroom were sundry wasps pinned down on white matting in blue and yellow frames. Their desiccated corpses as dried out as crackers. Her strongest passion was definitely for wasps: cuckoo wasps, great golden digger wasps, cicada killers, tarantula hawks, white-faced hornets, and yellow jackets. Her bee collection was much smaller, yet still impressive. Her honeybees hung directly above the head of her bed: a queen, five or six drones, and fifteen to twenty worker bees. They were all arranged in their hierarchies, with the queen at the apex of the pyramid.

Praxy could never get real thrilled over Liz's hobby of collecting and cataloging dead bugs. Whenever she was in Liz's room, it was inevitable that the topic of insects would come up. Praxy would try to fake some academic curiosity. Unfortunately, her politeness was generally mistaken for authentic interest, which caused Liz's face to glow with some strange faraway look. She became enraptured, talking at great length about the matriarchal politics of honeybees. She pointed out that the queen is the sole progenitor of the colony and that all the other bees are spawned from her eggs alone. She made a big point about the bee population consisting primarily of females. Even the workers are sterile females. She said it had something to do with not being fed royal jelly during their larvae stage. Liz explained how the workers feed it to the queen all her life. Praxy once asked her how royal jelly tasted. Liz looked at her oddly and said she didn't know. Praxy told her it sounded like it would taste real sweet. "Could be," Liz said patronizingly. "Whatever it tastes like, it's some real special stuff since the queen develops into a queen only because she diets on it."

"And the males?" Praxy asked. This provided Liz with the opportunity to lecture on how the male's role is drastically redefined in the honeybee world. She said there are a very small number of males, the drones, perhaps only a hundred in a hive that houses thousands of bees. Their primary function is to mate with the queen, and then die. "Just think of that, Praxy." Her face got all flushed. "What a commitment."

"It's a step further than your ordinary chivalry would go," Praxy quipped.

Praxy thought she saw Liz get some weird romantic glaze in her eyes, like going off and dying after mating was bordering on the mystical, or that this was the ultimate romantic gesture on the part of the male. Praxy remembered associating it with this thing she had heard about praying mantises, how the female bites off the male's head after mating. She wondered how the idea rested with Liz, but thought it better not to ask. Instead she made up some excuse to get Liz out of her room. So many insects in one place, though mummified insects, were starting to give her the creeps. Later she recalled having an itchy, burning feeling all over her skin that felt like thousands of tiny flea bites.

Apart from her obsession with bugs, Liz was pretty normal and even fun to be around. Praxy thought that Charlie might take an interest in Liz, since she was, like Charlie, a bookworm. She would devour a minimum of two novels a week. Also she was very cute. She was about five-five, and slender, but shapely. Her eyes were a lustrous gray-green and her lips large and full. But the cutest thing about her was her nose. It turned up slightly on the end, just enough to keep her thin glasses from sliding off whenever she bent over her books, or over her bugs.

Praxy had fixed Charlie up with her once on a double date with her and Billy. They had a great time talking about books and joking about school things, teachers and classes and such. But afterwards Charlie never asked Praxy a thing about Liz, and he never called Liz. He seemed to prefer just hanging around with her or with Billy.

Praxy could rely on Liz whenever she wanted to meet secretly with Billy. They had it all worked out. Since Liz rarely went out in the evenings during the school year, she agreed to "cover" for Praxy whenever she asked her to. Once the scam was in place, this meant if Liz's phone rang, she would have to answer it before her parents. And if it was Praxy's mother, Liz would tell her that Praxy was in the bathroom and that she would call her right back. Usually Praxy's mother just gave Liz a message, but if Praxy's mother wanted to talk with her, Liz would call Billy's house and tell Praxy to call her parents right away.

Before leaving the house, Praxy called Liz and told her to be prepared to run the scam, that she and Charlie were going over to Billy's to celebrate his promotion to Expert. Liz said she had her "covered." She had planned to stay home anyway to remount one of her wasp collections. She informed Praxy that she wanted to give her room a new look.

Praxy slowly steered her mother's Buick up to the curb. Since it was dark out, she had trouble picking out Billy's house. When she saw two motorcycles parked in front of an old brown duplex, she immediately recognized the long gray porch that spanned the front of the house. Its right side sagged noticeably, like an old ship keeled over to its port side.

The gravel popped under the tires as she swung the car into the drive. She got out and locked the door and then stepped around the back of the car to the front sidewalk. She felt the nippy air slide through her unbuttoned coat front as she mounted the porch stairs. On the porch, two doors opened to the street. The right one was Billy's neighbor's entrance. It had a storm door, or what was left of one. The bottom screen had a huge hole ripped through it about the size of a boot. On Billy's side was a gray door with half its paint flaked off.

Before she reached his door, Billy opened it and stepped out. He stood there smiling under a bare light bulb dangling from a wire overhead.

"Welcome," Billy grinned, raising his beer in a toast. "Come on in."

"Thanks."

Billy bowed and motioned Praxy in.

A Muddy Waters song boomed from the stereo. The music was so loud it actually rattled the windows.

"Well, Prax, here's to Billy Boy and Daytona," Charlie said.

"What? I can't hear you." Praxy walked over to the stereo and turned the volume down a few decibels.

"I said, here's to Billy and his career!" Charlie slurred out, waving a beer in front of him.

Praxy slipped out of her coat and looked around for some place to lay it. Before she could find a place to put it, Billy took it from her and dropped it in the chair.

"He's gonna kick some ass. Show "im how Ohio boys do it," Charlie screamed, his eyes noticeably red even in the dim light.

"Yeah, well, we'll have to see about that," Billy said. "Daytona's no friggin' hometown event. There'll be riders there from every part of the country, and most of them National Numbers."

Charlie tottered clumsily over to Praxy and draped his arm over her shoulder and around her neck, the arm with the beer can. She felt the heavy weight of his body leaning into her, so she placed her arm around his waist to steady him. His warm breath reeked of Frito chips and beer.

"So what! What if there are a few National Numbers there! They're just gonna have to move over and let you by!" Charlie slurred, spilling some beer down the front of Praxy's V-neck sweater.

"Charlie! You're spilling beer all over the place," she said, squirming free. "I'm gonna go home smellin' like I just returned from a beer bash." She pulled her sweater away from her body, trying to keep the beer from soaking into her blouse.

"I'm sorry, Prax. Let me get you a beer from the kitchen," Charlie said, embarrassed, veering off toward the dining room, like a fighter plane with its wing shot off, and then plunged through the plastic curtains that separated the kitchen from the dining room.

"God, how much did he drink?" Praxy asked, a little worried. "You think you can help me out of this thing?" she said, raising her arms so that Billy could slide her sweater off.

"Sure." He stepped behind her, pulled the sweater over her shoulders, and tossed it on the sofa next to her coat. Then he wrapped his arms around her waist, directly under her ribcage, and lowering his head, kissed her softly on her neck. Praxy felt his stiff hair brush against her cheek. Her entire body tingled like it had been zapped by a small electric current. She twisted around slowly in his arms and felt his hard, muscular chest chafe against her breasts. She raised her face to his and kissed him gently on the lips.

"Charlie will be all right. He's more excited about this weekend than I am," Billy said, drawing away.

"And you're not nervous about Sunday?" Her soft brown eyes looked searchingly into his.

"No, not really."

"Not at all?"

"Maybe a little. More nervous about setting my bike up for the right track conditions than anything else. And, maybe just a little friggin' worried about doing good, since this will be my first National," Billy admitted.

"Well, you just do your friggin' best and don't try and do any friggin' better than that," Praxy said, teasing Billy about his favorite expression.

"Here's that beer," Charlie said, emerging from the kitchen. "Still have a few cold ones left," he said, popping the tab. The beer foamed over the side of the can. He hurried it to his mouth, trying to trap it before it spilled onto the carpet. Some of the beer rushed down the side of the can onto his arm, trickling off his elbow onto the top of his shoe.

"God, Charlie, you're havin' a tough time tonight. Here, give me that a second," she laughed, pulling away from Billy and stepping over to Charlie and taking the beer from him. She set it down on top of a newspaper on the end table next to the sofa. "Let me get a dishtowel. Don't move. I'll be right back."

She disappeared into the kitchen and came out a second later with a plaid dishtowel. "Hold your arm out," she said as she began wiping off the beer. "Charlie, your parents are goin' to have an attack if you go home reeking of booze."

"No big deal. I'll just be grounded, that's all. They'll let me out on Thursday evenings to attend Alcoholics Anonymous. And on Sundays so I can eat Jesus at mass and have my sins forgiven."

"If you spill any more beer on the floor, Jesus won't be able to save you from my mom," Billy said half seriously.

"Come on, lighten up. This is supposed to be a celebration. Stay cool! I'm gonna get us some more beer," Charlie said, pivoting around in the direction of the kitchen. "This time I'll open it over the sink."

"He's gettin' pretty wasted, don't you think?" Praxy said, showing obvious concern.

"Yeah," Billy said, "you'd think he's the one who's gonna be racin' at Daytona. He's the one doin' all the celebrating."

The door of the refrigerator slammed shut, rattling the trays and bottles inside. Then Praxy and Billy heard two tabs pop. A second later Charlie stumbled through the curtained doorway. As he came through, the plastic fabric wrapped around his face temporarily blinding him. "Who turned off the lights!" he said laughing loudly.

Billy stepped over and pulled the curtain off his head. Then he took one of the beers from him and raised it, touching his can lightly against Charlie's. "To a great year!"

"And to the three of us!" Charlie said, putting his arm around Billy and then reeling around to Praxy. "Pals forever. What do yuh say, Prax?" Charlie's arm shot up in the air in a toast.

Praxy watched beer splash out of his can onto his shirt and onto Billy. She just laughed again and shook her head. Charlie was incorrigible, a hopeless case. She picked up the dishtowel and threw it at him. It wrapped around his neck. "This time clean yourself up. You're becoming a pig."

She grabbed a beer from the end table and then stepped between them, throwing her arms around both of their necks and squeezing them tightly. "To the three Musketeers. Soul brothers and soul sister forever," she laughed, her eyes a sparkling opalescent under the soft glow of the ceiling light. "Like in that poem, you know, the one about two souls as one. Remember, Mrs. Graystone illustrated the idea on the board for us? One soul is the center foot of the compass, and the other the outer foot that forms the perfect circle."

"Yeah, I remember. John Donne. Pretty cool, Praxy," Charlie said.

"I don't think you need that beer, Prax. Sounds pretty friggin' wacko to me," Billy interjected.

"Come on, Prax! Let's try it. Let's show Billy how it works. The three of us as one. We'll be one big soul person! Here, you be the center," Charlie said, grabbing Praxy's arms and dragging her to the center of the living room.

Praxy felt silly. She had only brought up the idea as a kind of joke, nothing more. Now Charlie was wild about illustrating it to Billy. Billy probably didn't remember the poem at all, and even if he did, it was nothing to get ecstatic over.

"Billy, you stand here, to the right of Praxy," Charlie said excitedly, giving Billy a clumsy push. "And I'll stand over here on the left. Now, Praxy, don't move. Billy, lean into her with both of your arms over her right shoulder. And I'll do the same." Charlie spun over to her other side, almost losing his footing. "Okay, now we got it."

"Charlie, this is friggin' crazy. We look like Siamese triplets, not a compass, or whatever it is you're tryin' to make us into."

"Just be cool, dude. Hang with me. Here, I have to put my arm over yours and grab your arm up high to stabilize myself. Got it? Now you do the same."

"Now what do you want me to do?" Praxy laughed. "I feel pretty tangled up. I'm not sure this is what Donne had in mind as soul partners."

"Screw Donne. We're improvin' on his idea. Look, Prax. Just hang loose. We need to make a complete circle on the carpet, so move your two legs close together. You're the pivot point. Okay?"

"Yeah, I got it. I'm not sure I can do it without fallin' over though, not with you two leaning against me with all your weight."

"You can do it. Just shift your feet around slowly, keeping your legs as close together as you can. Now, Billy, we need to stretch our legs out some, so they resemble the legs of a compass."

"Charlie, I don't want to blow a hole in your balloon, but a compass doesn't have three legs," Praxy said. "At least not the ones I used to use in geometry class."

"This one does. Because our souls are three, not two. Like I said, we're modifying an old idea. And if you want to make our three souls one, then do what I say. Ready?"

114

"Okay, chief. Whatever the wise master requests." Praxy could hardly contain her laughter. She had to hold her breath to keep from bursting out. Charlie was so serious, and Billy was just going along with it all to humor them.

"Okay, start rotating, will you?"

"Ready, guru? Here goes!" She tried slowly rotating her feet, pressing her left sole against her right sole and using her heel as the pivot point. She had only managed to turn two or three degrees when she felt their two bodies stiffen and then sway a little before locking. Their feet stuck to the carpet like Velcro. "You're going to have to move your feet with mine if you want this to work," she yelled. It was like winding up a spring, and she had the sensation that at any moment the spring was going to unwind and the three of them were going to be spun off in opposite directions. To prevent this from happening, she twisted her upper body more to help them move with her.

"So what's next, Charlie?" Billy chuckled. "You want us to do Om chants?"

Then suddenly Praxy felt her body give way under the weight of Charlie who was leaning awkwardly into her. The next thing she knew she was in a full tilt. As her feet became uprooted from the carpet, she was flung sideways like a railcar bumped off its track. The three of them toppled to the floor, with Charlie flat on his back and Praxy directly on top of him, her face inches from his. Billy got up quickly and stood over them, shaking his head at Charlie's craziness.

115

Charlie was laughing wildly. Praxy started to lift herself off him, and without realizing it, he put his arms around her and drew her closer to him. She felt his chest rise and fall underneath her, in rhythm with the slow blues song playing on the stereo. She looked at his hair spread out over the carpet. It was longer than Billy's and much thinner and much straighter. She imagined it as soft as robin's down and wondered momentarily what it would feel like to run her fingers through it.

"Hey, soul partner," Charlie said effusively.

Praxy looked into his eyes. They were blue like Billy's, but different. They were readable, no more enigmatic or mysterious than a thermometer. They allowed access. And she noticed that behind the gaiety they reflected outwardly, there was a more serious feeling being communicated, something she thought she had seen before. She listened as James Cotton bellowed out some lines from "Sugar Sweet." "Yes she's my baby, she's my baby, can't you see? Well, I can't call her sugar, sugar never was so sweet."

"Yeah, soul partner. Let's not let this soul partner stuff carry us away." Praxy's words had a noticeably nervous strain to them, like they were coming from a stretched vocal cord. Charlie must have sensed it, because she immediately felt the muscles in his hands relax. She lifted herself off him and then stood up, smoothing the wrinkles out of her blouse.

Billy had not moved. He stood there with this half-amused expression. For a second Praxy thought she caught a fleeting glimpse of something else, not in his eyes exactly, but more like a shadow that stole fleetingly over his face and then quickly vanished.

Charlie got up slowly and wobbled over toward the end table. His leg bumped into it. sending an empty beer can rolling to the floor. He stooped over and picked it up and set it back on the table. Then he grabbed up his brown aviation jacket from where he had tossed it on the back of the sofa. "Think before I head for home it might be a good idea to take a walk around the block, clear some of the fumes out of my head. Anyone want to go along?" Charlie said sheepishly, lumbering over to the front door. He grabbed the doorknob and leaned against the door.

"I think maybe I should be goin', too," Praxy said. "School tomorrow, you know. And anyway, Billy, you need to get a good night's rest since you're leavin' early in the morning."

"That's no reason to go. I'll be able to sleep on the way down to Daytona. Chuck Jarvis, my mechanic, will be doin' the drivin'."

"Well, I'm gonna take a walk, then get on home. Thanks for the buzz, Billy. See yuh at school tomorrow, Prax." Charlie opened the front door, and a cold draft of air shot in. "And, Billy, don't forget to pick me up at the airport Thursday night."

"Hold on a second, Charlie. I think I could use a little fresh air myself. Let me just say good-bye to Praxy and I'll be right out."

"Sure." Charlie glanced over at Praxy. "See you, soul partner." Then he pulled the door closed behind him.

Though the CD had ended, Praxy couldn't get the music out of her head. "Yes, she's my baby, she's my baby, can't you see? But I can't call her sugar, sugar never was so sweet."

"I just want to make sure he sobers up some before he takes off," Billy said. "Maybe I can talk him into leavin' his bike out back. I can chain it to mine after I give him a ride home."

"That's a good idea, Billy," she said, and then paused for a few seconds before continuing. "So, it looks like good-bye for awhile. How long you gonna be gone?" She blushed some as she heard her voice faltering.

"Well, after the Daytona race, Chuck and I will load up and head West for the Sacramento Mile. We'll be out that way for a few weeks because of the Pomona and San Jose races. Then we work our way back. There are a couple of races in the Southwest, like the Oklahoma National, before we get back here and to the half-miles at Louisville and Lima. We'll be back in the area in early May."

"May? That's two months." She hadn't imagined he would be gone quite so long. She felt a tightness in her stomach. "You'll write, won't you?"

"Well, I'm not too good about writing."

"Then you'll have to call." Praxy arched her eyebrows coquettishly, and then fixed her big brown eyes on his, hoping to get a commitment.

"Not every friggin' day, that's for sure. But I'll call every now and then."

"Well, I friggin' hope so," she teased. She put her arms around him and leaned her head against his chest.

118

She felt Billy's hand move lightly, caressingly, over her hair in and out of her curls. She lifted her head from where it lay against his soft cotton shirt. "You be careful now," she whispered, pulling back so she could look him fully in the eyes.

"Don't you…"

"Friggin'" she interjected.

"Yeah, friggin' worry about me," Billy laughed. "I'll be fine."

"I never worry about you. You're too damn cool for anyone to worry about," she kidded. "Now if you're gonna take a walk with Charlie, you better not leave him standin' out there in the cold too long."

"Oh yeah, Charlie. I almost forgot." He gave her a kiss and then reeled around looking for his leather jacket. He grabbed it up from the floor near the stereo and slipped it on. "Bye." He kissed her again and then opened the door and stepped out onto the porch.

As soon as the door closed behind him, it flew open again and he lunged back inside. He caught her up in his arms and kissed her once more. "I just wanted to say good-bye one last time." She felt her body hanging limply, and then he suddenly released her and spun around quickly and rushed out the door, slamming it shut behind him.

"Good luck!" she shouted. It was too late. He was already too far away to hear her.

Praxy searched for her coat in the dim light of the living room. Until tonight, she had never been alone in Billy's house. From outside, the house looked larger. Inside it was different, smaller and stuffy. The furniture looked as old as the house itself. In the center of the dining room was a large, bulky table with a gaudily carved pedestal base of leaves and berries. The dining room chairs had faded green velvet upholstery, and one of them had a slit in the seat with cotton candy-like padding protruding from it. The black vinyl sofa in the living room didn't match any of the other furniture, especially the light oak-colored end tables. The whole house seemed so gloomy inside. The dim living room and dining room lights only added to the prevailing gloom. At first she thought maybe the weak lighting was due to old wiring in the house, and then she remembered something her father had said about using small watt bulbs for the outdoor lights. The smaller bulbs used less electricity and were therefore less costly.

Praxy picked up her red wool coat from the chair by the front window. Though it was warm inside the house, she felt chilled. She slipped the coat on and fastened a couple of its large brass buttons. Standing alone in the living room, she began to feel odd, as though she were an intruder. The house seemed so strange to her. There was certainly nothing about the place that reminded her of her own home.

She collected the empty beer cans and deposited them in the kitchen sink to drain. When she returned to the living room, she gathered up the newspaper from the end table and folded it neatly and set it back down. Then she went over to the stereo and began picking up loose CD albums from the carpet. She placed the CDs in the fruit crate table that was used for a stereo table. Nothing about this house seemed right.

And Billy's mother, what was she like? Praxy had never met her. She wondered if she looked like Billy or if Billy took after his father. Then a thought entered her mind. There must be a picture of his mother somewhere. Why not look? It wasn't really snooping or anything like that. If Billy were here, she could ask him to see a picture. Anyway, it would just take a second to peek.

To the left of the dining room was a narrow hall that led to two bedrooms and a bathroom at the far end of the hall. She opened the first door on the left and walked in. The room was dark except for some faint light from outside the window that fell on the various objects in the room, giving them a kind of other-worldliness. Next to the window was a large double-bed with a tall headboard. The bed was high off the floor and covered with what appeared to be a silver bedspread. Against the wall, directly in front of the bed, stood a dresser with a heart-shaped mirror.

Praxy picked up a large picture in a silver frame from the dresser top. At first she could not make out the details, but when she turned the photo toward the window, she was able to trace out two faces. She moved closer to the window so she could hold the picture directly in the light. Right outside, as though it had fallen from the sky and now sat resting on the neighbor's roof, was the biggest moon she had ever seen. She held the picture frame up to the moon, like an offering. In the photo were two figures, one a young woman in a dark dress with a white lace collar, and the other a man in a military uniform, but with Billy's face! It was an old photo, perhaps taken twenty years ago. They were a handsome couple, and happy too, if you can judge by a photo.

Billy rarely ever mentioned his parents. All she knew of his father was that he had left Billy's mother and then died somewhere out West. And his mother, well, she had a night-shift job in some plastics company. That was about the sum of what she knew.

She looked at the woman in the picture she held in her hands. She was pretty, but not beautiful. Her hair was dark brown and she had a small mouth, a bit too small, and a slightly inclined chin. There was also something timid about her eyes.

Praxy walked back to the dresser and set the picture down in its place. Though it had been years since Billy's father left Billy's mother, she still kept their picture next to her bed. Had she really loved him that much? And Billy's father, how had he felt about her? Probably not the same, since he was the one who left. Had she become too old? A bit too matronly? This wasn't like life in the bee queendom, Praxy thought, remembering Liz and her bees. No, bees didn't know beans about growing old and unattractive. It was something every middle-aged woman feared though. Some wrinkles around the eyes, a little weight about the waist, sagging breasts, and you were history.

She gave a sigh of relief as she left the bedroom. As she passed by the kitchen, she heard the sink dripping. She pushed through the plastic curtains. The constant dripping had left a yellow stain on the grayish-white porcelain. On the scuffed-up linoleum floor in front of the sink was a worn spot about a yard wide, a sad metaphor, she thought, for this poor woman's life.

Standing in the living room once again, she felt the scratchy newness of her wool collar chafe her neck. She withdrew a pair of white angora gloves from the side pockets of her coat and slipped them on. The gloves were a present from her father. They were identical to the ones he had given her mother the year before, except for the color. Inside the gloves, her hands felt warm and secure.

She placed her gloved hands on the hard metal doorknob and turned it gently. Before opening the front door, she took one last look at the living room, dining room, and plastic curtains. Suddenly a feeling of sorrow welled up inside. Not for Billy exactly, yet part of it was for him. Her thoughts were mostly on the young woman in the photo. She must have had dreams too. And now?

Closing the door softly behind her, Praxy stepped out into the cool, refreshing night air. She inhaled deeply and felt the thin air burn her lungs. Tilting her head back, she stared up at the Milky Way, where a spiraling ball of white whirled diffusely out from its center. Across the night's canopy, stars spread out as profusely as an adolescent's dreams. Standing on the sidewalk next to the curb, she was free and young and full of life. The heaviness that had bound her moments before seemed to fall away, and now she felt as light and unshackled as a moonbeam. Gazing upwards, she even thought she heard the spangled night whispering promises to her.

CHAPTER TEN

As planned, on Thursday night Billy and Chuck arrived in Bradley's shop van at the Daytona Airport to pick up Charlie. The van and mechanic were part of the deal. Bradley had insisted on providing Billy with transportation, a tuner, and a Harley XR 750. He had also given Chuck the shop credit card to pay for motel expenses.

On the way in from the airport, Charlie huddled on the floor in a small space behind the passenger seat. Chuck and Billy had managed to cram into the back of the van two motorcycles, five extra tires, a five-drawer tool-box, two five-gallon cans for fuel, a case of racing oil, a box of spare parts, three aluminum lawn chairs, three sleeping bags, a center stand, some blankets, and two or three other boxes of miscellaneous items.

So, Charlie was finally in Daytona. The big weekend had arrived, and everything had gone as smoothly as planned. After the "celebration" on Wednesday night, Billy had taken Charlie home and helped him up the front lawn to his porch. All the lights in the house were out except the porch light and the light in the foyer. His parents apparently were asleep. Once inside, he crawled up the steps on all fours to keep from losing his balance and stumbling and crashing into the stair wall. When he finally reached the top, he stood up and felt his way along the wall to his bedroom door.

Inside his room, he toppled into bed, striking his head soundly on the headboard. He thought for sure the noise would wake his parents, so he slipped furtively under the covers and lay there without stirring. The next thing he heard was the alarm clock going off and his mother calling him down to breakfast. At the kitchen table, his mother and father were ghostly adumbrations chatting back and forth in what seemed like a foreign language. He stared into his cereal bowl and concentrated on the puffed kernels of sugar-coated wheat eddying around and around in his bowl.

In the van Chuck had turned the music up. There was a Patsy Cline song playing that Charlie vaguely recognized. Chuck was a country boy at heart, though he had spent nearly all of his forty-some-odd years in the city. He looked like a caricature of the Marlboro cowboy in the cigarette ads, but much skinnier. He was tall and wiry and chain-smoked Camel cigarettes, and his skin looked as course as a lizard's. He always wore, it seemed, a pair of Levi's a size too small and two or three inches too short.

"I'm crazy, crazy for feelin' so lonely. I'm crazy, crazy for feelin' so blue. I knew you'd love me as long as you wanted. And then someday you'd leave me for somebody new." Chuck whistled along with the tape. Charlie remembered the song from the movie *The Patsy Cline Story*. Trying to stretch out, he pushed against the back of Billy's seat, but the soles of his shoes struck the front tire of the Harley, so he just closed his eyes, leaned his head back, and listened to the whine of the tires against the pavement. It seemed to be the perfect backdrop for the song. After the song ended, the words kept turning over and over again in his mind: I'm crazy for tryin', I'm crazy for cryin', and I'm crazy for lovin' you." Chuck had turned on the heater and the back of the van was now warm and filled with country music and the pungent smoke of Chuck's Camel cigarettes.

"Billy, what are the plans for tomorrow?" Charlie shouted above the music.

"What?"

Chuck reached over to the center of the dash and turned down the music. Then he lowered the window and flipped his cigarette out. Charlie felt a cold stream of air rush in.

"I was wondering what your plans are for tomorrow," Charlie repeated.

"Well, we was thinkin' about headin' out real early in the morning for the pro race up near the Georgia line. They're payin' a pretty good purse, about five thousand for first place. There'll be a whole lot of Experts and National Numbers up there, guys who came in early for the Daytona race."

"Great! I can't wait!" Charlie said, wiggling around some and feeling his tailbone chafe against the hard floor. The sleeping bag he was sitting on felt pathetically thin against the floor's metal ribbing.

"If nothin' else, it gives us a chance to dial in the bike," Chuck said matter-of-factly. "Down here, we're dealin' with more humidity and barometric pressure. That's probably gonna mean changin' jets in the carbs."

The van slowed abruptly, made a sharp left, and then squeaked and bounced into a parking lot. The bike and Charlie rose a few inches into the air as the van struck what appeared to be a speed bump.

"Sorry. Didn't see it," Chuck said.

The van rolled to a stop next to a pulsating neon sign. Staccato flashes of red and blue light shot through the windshield into the back of the van.

"Well, we're here. Billy, why don't yuh take Charlie's suitcase in and lock up the van," Chuck said, tossing Billy the motel keys. Charlie can come with me to the office. Since we'll be here a few days, I don't think it's a good idea to try and sneak "im in."

Charlie followed Chuck over to a small, well-lit room at the foot of the stairs that led up to a redwood balcony. Chuck talked to a young clerk through a small round hole in the plate-glass window. Right below the hole was a stainless steel metal drawer for money and documents. It was apparently a night security measure that the motel franchise had adopted to discourage robberies.

A cold breeze suddenly picked up, blowing a few dead leaves across the parking lot. They made a scraping sound as they slid over the pavement past Charlie and Chuck. It was no warmer here than it was the night at Billy's house, Charlie reflected with a shiver. He recalled Praxy teasing them about a frost warning. Wouldn't that be their luck?

Charlie zipped up his jacket so that the collar was tight around his neck. He gazed in the direction of the broad boulevard in front of the motel. The place reminded him of scenes he had seen in movies of Las Vegas nightlife. Street lamps mounted on tall aluminum poles poured their liquid brilliance down on the shiny asphalt, while flashing neon signs bathed the night in iridescent colors. The parking lot, the motel, the plaza across the boulevard, the cars streaming by, everything, seemed wet and glittering in bright rainbow hues.

Then from farther down the boulevard he heard the deep thunder of motorcycle engines, their gutted exhaust pipes blatting out sharp desultory explosions. Coming into view were fifteen to twenty low-slung choppers. Charlie judged by the rake and length of their extended front forks that it would take half the motel parking lot for them to make a complete turn. The gang was decked out in wild costumes, black leather and Levi's jackets adorned with metal chains, fringe, and other colorful paraphernalia. As the bikes came to a stop at the intersection, his eyes strained in an effort to see what was written on the back of their jackets. He could make out "Devil's Disciples" in large white letters drawn out in something that looked like gothic script. Underneath the letters was a skull with a Nazi helmet. The helmet had wings coming out of the side and a motorcycle wheel under it. A couple of other guys had on helmets with spikes, like those worn by the Germans in World War I, and one biker even had on what looked like a safari hat. As they tore away from the intersection, two guys in the back of the pack spun their tires and gave out some loud unintelligible whoops. What a spirited and colorful group of misfits, Charlie thought.

Chuck took the receipt out of the stainless steel drawer and slipped it into his jeans pocket. "Sounds like half of them bikes could use a good tunin'," he laughed.

"Of course them numb-nuts wouldn't know the difference between a engine runnin' on one cylinder or on two. That's 'cause their brains is sputterin' along most the time on a dead cylinder."

"Hey, Chuck, I thought you used to be a Hell's Angel yourself, before becoming a wrench at Bradley's," Charlie kidded.

"Can't stand the sons-of-bitches! About two months ago, one of them scuzzy bastards was out back of The Main Street Tavern lookin' my bike over real close, like with his hands. He was tryin' to unscrew my tac cable. I asked the bastard what he was doin', and he smiled at me with his scuzzy teeth showin' and just walked away like he didn't owe nobody no explanation."

"So, what did you do?"

"I asked him again what he thought he was doin' foolin' around with my bike. Well, he stopped and turned around. Then he pushed the front of his jacket open so I could see this gun he'd shoved underneath his belt. Was a 38 or bigger. I'm no damn fool. I just let the jerk go."

"I can understand that," Charlie said, rubbing his hands together to warm them.

"It's guys like that that ruin it for guys like us. That's why bikers get a bad rep."

"Hey, like they say. It's a free country."

"Free, my ass."

"Hey, you guys gonna stand out in the parkin' lot all night!" Billy yelled from up on the balcony. "Why don't we clean up and then go out and grab somethin' to eat?"

Charlie hoped that things would turn out better than they had yesterday at the Valdosta county short-track. The race ended up being a grand disappointment. Billy had turned in the third fastest qualifying time. Chuck worked frantically, re-jetting the carburetor and setting up the suspension and the gearing. Getting to the final looked like a sure thing. Of course almost anything could happen in a heat race. And it did. Three laps into the heat, after a wobbly tire-spinning start, Billy moved from near last place to third. Two laps later, he closed in right behind the first-place rider. Then going into turn four, a first-year Expert from Texas tried to dive under him but instead clipped Billy's rear tire. Billy's bike high-sided, and he went sailing over the handlebars. Fortunately he came down softly on his shoulder in the loose cushion up by the guardrail. The Texan slid down gracefully, his bike enveloped in a cloud of thick dust. Billy couldn't make the restart because his forks were knocked out of alignment and his handlebars were bent like a pretzel. Charlie was livid, and Chuck was fit to be tied. They watched the Texan restart and win his heat. Billy didn't say a word. He just dusted off his leathers while Chuck pushed his bike back toward the pits, grumbling about the "crazy son-of-bitchin' cowboy." Billy quietly set to work aligning his forks while Chuck tried to change the twisted handlebars. Chuck couldn't hold on to his wrenches. He kept dropping them in the grass while he groaned under his breath about how he'd like to take the handlebars and straighten them out on the cowboy's head. Charlie just followed behind Chuck, picking up his wrenches each time they fell in the grass.

That was yesterday, Charlie thought, hurrying along beside Billy. Today was what really mattered. The Daytona National! His insides tingled. Any minute now his friend Billy Solinski would be out on the track qualifying for a position in one of the four heat races that would determine what riders made the final event.

"Okay, Billy, I'm gonna have yuh on the clock, so when yuh come out of turn four, if I don't think your time will get yuh a front-row startin' position, I'll wave yuh off. Just watch me as yuh exit turn four." Chuck handed Billy his helmet. "Let's hope today goes better than last night!"

"Okay. Don't forget to hold your cap out where I can see it." Billy pulled on his helmet and began pushing the bike toward the stadium gate. The metal shoe on his left foot caused him to slip now and then as he shoved the bike through the wet grass.

"I'll make certain yuh see it," Chuck said, patting the Cincinnati Reds baseball cap he had on. Billy threw his leg over the bike and sat down firmly on the seat. Chuck grabbed the fiberglass tail section of the bike and leaned into it, pushing it across the track into the infield grass near the start/finish line where a slew of other bikes were in line waiting to qualify.

Billy nodded and then pulled down his visor. Chuck then gave the bike a shove and ran behind it, pushing down on the tail. Standing up on the foot pegs, Billy came down flatly on the thin seat with his full one hundred and sixty-five pounds. The bike coughed and sputtered and then exploded into a deep-throated roar as yellow flames shot out of the exhaust. He rolled the

131

throttle back, and the engine swallowed air and thundered back heavy pulsating notes. Billy steered the bike to the starting line near the officials' tower while Chuck strutted after him like an old rooster.

Chuck had told Charlie to go over to turn four in the infield, and he would meet him there as soon as Billy was out on the track. The officials were sending two bikes out at a time, separated by the distance of a straightaway. He could feel the ground shake under him as the bikes flashed by him. If a rider didn't feel good about his lap time, he could wave off as he exited turn four, right before he crossed the finish line. Riders really had no accurate way of knowing their times. It was just a feeling. If they overshot a turn or bobbled some, they would most likely wave off, though a small slip-up didn't always mean that their overall time was poor. Chuck had devised a way of letting Billy know his time. All it required was a stopwatch and a baseball cap.

Charlie had spent a little time in the pit area before coming into the infield. He was amazed at the number of bikes and riders. He had never seen so many motorcycles assembled in one spot. According to Chuck, there were approximately 160 Experts signed up, half of them National Numbers. For Billy to enter the heat races, he had to be among the top forty-eight qualifiers. That meant his lap time had to be faster than the lap times of 112 other Experts. The thought made Charlie pale. Was Billy that good?

From where he stood in the infield, he could see that the stadium was nearly filled. It had been constructed above a brick wall that enclosed the track.

The spectators looked down into a sort of bowl-shaped arena. Their elevated position far above the track made Charlie think of the Roman Coliseum and the gladiators. He wondered if in Roman times the walls of the coliseum displayed advertisements. What would they have advertised? Spiked maces for pulverizing linden shields? High-tech cast-iron swords, guaranteed never to break or your money back? The walls here were pasted over with ads for Budweiser and Miller beers, Kendal and Castrol oils, Champion spark plugs, Goodyear tires, and, of course, Camel cigarettes. Camel was the main sponsor of the Grand National races. For this reason, the nationals were called the Camel Pro Series. As they pulled into the stadium, Charlie remembered seeing a billboard with a huge grinning camel face that had a cigarette dangling from its thick brown lips. How that mug would sell any cigarettes was anyone's guess.

It looked like it was Billy's turn to go out. Charlie watched across the infield as Chuck gave Billy's bike a hard shove. After it started, he turned around quickly and ran toward Charlie, his stopwatch dangling from a cord around his wrist. Billy lined up behind six bikes, each waiting its turn to be flagged onto the track.

Charlie had been trying to listen to the times announced as the riders crossed the finish line on their qualifying lap. Each one was given one warm up lap and then put on the clock on his second lap. Charlie had heard times in the high and middle 17s. He remembered Chuck saying that last year's track record was 17.1 seconds.

"Damn tracks gettin' slick," Chuck said, a little out of breath from his run across the infield. "Good thing Billy's number isn't higher."

"His number?" Charlie asked.

"Yeah, they gotta pick a number from a box so no one can claim an unfair advantage if the track changes, which it always does. Right now it's slickin' up some. It's that damn sandy soil. If the track's not watered down right, then it gets slippery as hell out there."

Chuck held the stopwatch close to his face while he focused his eyes on an object near the start/finish line. Then, pivoting on his heels, he spun around and focused on one of the bright orange cones between turns three and four. They had been set in the track near the infield guardrail to keep riders from laying down rubber in the tight corners around the rail. If this happened early in the event, the track would have a black narrow groove around it, making passing outside the narrow band difficult. Whenever this happened, the result was sixteen bikes freight-training around a narrow black ribbon.

"Tryin' to get times on the other bikes?" Charlie asked.

"Yeah, yuh can help me some. Listen closely for the times on the next two bikes, just in case I don't hear nothin'. I'll hit the start button when they cross over the line, and then the stop button when they're in the middle of turn three and four. If they have good times, say in the mid or lower 17s, I'll know what Billy needs when he gets to the same spot between turns three and four." Chuck was all concentration now. With one eye closed, he aimed his stopwatch at the start/finish line. His thumb was bent over the large red button on the top of the watch.

Though it was only about ten o'clock, it was already muggy. Charlie slipped out of his leather jacket and tossed it on the grass near his feet. He listened closely for the time on the bike that had just crossed the start/finish.

"Did yuh get the time?" Chuck asked.

"17.46," Charlie said.

"That's a damn good time. I got him at 13.25 in the middle of the turn. I'll use that time as a reference. Here," he said, taking off his cap and handing it to Charlie. "Yuh stand right over there close to the track, and when Billy comes out of turn four, if I point to my head, you wave the hat up and down like crazy so Billy sees it. Okay?"

"Yeah, sure!" Charlie could feel his heart pounding madly.

"Okay!" yelled Chuck. "Get ready. He's goin' out."

Charlie felt short of breath as he watched Billy pull onto the track. So this was it! The real thing!

He listened breathlessly as Billy's bike shot down the back stretch. Billy leaned the bike low and gracefully into turn three and then rolled the throttle back fully in the middle of the corner. As he exited the turn, he lifted his left leg onto the foot peg and slid back on the seat, shifting his weight to the rear wheel to make it dig in and hook up with the loose, sandy soil. The official waved the green flag in front of him as he crossed the start/finish. He was on the clock!

Billy dove into turn one and came down on the gas shortly after he started his slide. From his rear wheel, a thick spray of wet, gritty sand shot upward, forming a lofty rooster tail way above the outer guardrail. When he came onto the back stretch, he bent forward, his chest pressed down firmly against the gas tank. Charlie felt the ground shake and his whole body tremble as Billy's bike thundered down the back stretch. As he entered turn three, Billy slid forward on the seat, pitching the bike low to the ground and sideways, turning his handlebars in the direction of his slide toward the wall. Immediately he was back on the throttle, his rear tire splattering the wall with wet sand.

With the baseball cap held tightly in his hand behind him, Charlie turned quickly toward Chuck and looked for a signal. It was now or never! Chuck's thin grizzled face looked up from the stopwatch at Charlie and beamed. Charlie cocked his ear in the direction of the loudspeaker. Time 17.29. He tossed Chuck's baseball hat high into the air.

Chuck, unable to control himself, rushed over to Charlie, grabbing him by the arms and swinging him around in a circle, dancing and laughing like a lunatic. "Holy Jesus Christ! Can yuh believe it? Got to be one of the fastest times so far!" Chuck was ecstatic.

"That'll get him a front row start then?"

"Yuh damn well bet it will!" Chuck shouted jubilantly. He pulled a greasy rag out of the rear pocket of his jeans and bent over and dusted off his cowboy boots. Then he and Charlie scrambled across the track toward the pit area behind the stadium wall.

Billy had just passed through the stadium gates into the pit area. He coasted up to the rear of the van as Charlie and Chuck came running up to him.

"How'd I do?" Billy asked, removing his helmet and slipping off his gloves. He handed them to Chuck. He was still straddling his motorcycle.

"17.29!" Charlie shouted out.

"It's one of the fastest times so far. Yuh really screwed it on comin' out of the corners. Looked like the high line worked. Yuh had a hell of a rooster tail flyin' off your back tire," Chuck beamed.

"Yeah, I pushed the bike deep into the cushion to grab some traction. I thought I'd take my chances up high. Looks like it paid off. The tires are working great."

"How long till your heat?" Charlie asked.

"Well, they can't post the heat races until the time trials are over. That'll be a while."

Chuck was already fumbling around in the toolbox. "How's the suspension feel?" He was looking for the wheel wrench. He would need to flip the tires over before the heat race. "I'm gonna be safe and change the air filter."

"Suspension's fine," Billy said, stepping over to the back of the van.

"Hey, man, you're smokin' out there." A young guy in red, white, and black racing leathers limped up to Billy, dragging his right leg behind him like it had an iron ball attached to it. Billy was trying to wiggle out of his leathers.

"Thanks. Hope the track doesn't change much,'" Billy replied warmly. "Have you gone out yet?"

"Yeah, but I had a little problem hookin' up. Slipped off the groove between two and three and lost a little time, but I think I'll qualify. Should have probably gone up higher in the loose stuff, but I didn't have the right tires for it. The cushion seemed to be workin' for you."

"Yeah, well, I thought down by the pylons it had gotten a bit too greasy, so I took a chance and high-lined it."

"You got any tie-downs I could borrow? My number plate's about ready to fly off."

"Yeah, sure." Billy walked over to the toolbox and grabbed some white plastic strips out of the top drawer. "Here," he said, giving them a toss.

"Thanks, and good luck, not that you'll need it, not if you burn up the track like you just did." He nodded to Charlie and Chuck, "Catch yuh all later," and then hobbled back toward his van.

"Who's that?" Charlie asked.

"Robby Johnson. Just turned Expert this year, too. Damn good on the half-mile tracks," Billy replied, reaching in the back of the van and snatching up an old T-shirt from a sack of rags and wiping the sweat from his forehead. He laid the shirt over the seat of the Harley, and then pulled his leathers down around his waist so he could cool off more.

"What's wrong with his leg?" Charlie asked. "It looks like he's just draggin' it along with him."

"He is. It's plastic, from the knee down."

"You're kiddin'," Charlie said. He had an incredulous look on his face, like a small child who had just discovered real guns actually hurt people.

"Got it smashed when he was a kid. Right in front of his house. Ran out into the street to get a stupid little sponge football his sister had thrown over his head. And SMASH! Just like that, this car smacked into him, tearin' his leg clean off. The car hit him so hard that he ended up on his front lawn."

"Wow! How can he race with one leg? I mean, you'd think it would be dangerous racing with a leg missing. How does he keep the plastic leg on the foot peg? Doesn't it slip off?"

"He has a special set-up that keeps it from slidin' off. It's some kind of metal band that wraps over the toe of his right boot. Seems to work fine. He finished third last year at the regional half-mile in New York. It was a big race, a Junior invitational with Junior riders from all over the country."

Charlie couldn't believe it. Robby Johnson was his own age. What balls! Racing a motorcycle with only one leg! And qualifying at Daytona! The world was full of incredible individuals. He suddenly felt proud to have Billy as his friend. Billy had the talent and the guts to make it on his own. And if he failed, he'd accept that too. The big accomplishments in life took risks, but there weren't a whole lot of people willing to gamble. No, the average guy just looked for an easy way to cruise through life, instead of looking for the "roads less traveled by." Few, it was sure, set their goals as high as Billy. The stakes were too risky and the outcome too uncertain.

139

Uncertainty was a bogeyman—for most people. Billy was the exception. Being at Daytona and competing against the best racers in the world, and qualifying among the best of the best, at eighteen, was a feat on par with the greatest of Charlie's only to be dreamed of accomplishments.

"They're gonna be postin' the heat races," Chuck said, laying down an open-end wrench. "Think I'll walk over and see if your heat's posted yet." He snatched up a ratchet and finished tightening the spark plug in the cylinder head and then tossed it with a clang back into the toolbox. After looking around momentarily for something to clean his greasy hands on, he picked up the same T-shirt Billy had used to wipe his face.

The sun resting on the roof of the stadium had started its slow, scorching descent. The temperature had risen considerably since the time trials, requiring the water truck to make two trips to the track. This was its final trip before the first heat race. As it exited through the stadium gates, the red Ford tractor, which had been tailing it, made its final laps, dragging behind it six feet of mesh fencing weighted down with a heavy log. The tractor's job was to level the track, pulling the smooth sand from the cushion down onto the track's surface.

Billy pulled his leathers back on. His heat race was the first heat of the four. The stands ringing the track were completely filled now. Except for the squelching heat, it was a perfect day for spectating. The sky was a powdery blue, and a few thin white clouds high up in the sky wafted picturesquely by.

Charlie strutted proudly behind Billy and Chuck as Chuck pushed the Rotax through the stadium gate to the start/finish line. The fluorescent orange, white, and blue on the tank and tailpiece matched Billy's leathers. Harley-Davidson was painted in large black letters on the side of the tank. Charlie thought this was odd, since the engine was built by Rotax, an Austrian company, and the frame by Knight Racing Frames. He once had asked Billy why a Rotax was being passed off as a Harley-Davidson. Billy told him that Harley-Davidson didn't have a small competitive motorcycle so the company purchased engines from CanAm. That way Harley-Davidson would have a short-track bike. Charlie laughed secretly as he thought about the guys at Bradley's who teased him about riding a Honda. What a bunch of jerks! Not one short-track bike out there was built in the good ole USA.

"Good luck," Charlie said, giving Billy a small jab on his arm.

"Thanks," Billy replied. "I'm glad you're here."

"Ladies and gentlemen, will you please rise for the playing of the national anthem," the loudspeakers crackled. Charlie watched the people in the stands rise, and the riders on the track turn and face the flag hanging limply from a tall white pole in the infield. He put his hand over his heart and listened as the words blared from a scratchy recording of the national anthem. Looking out of the corner of his eye at Billy, Charlie noticed that his attention was not focused on the Stars and Stripes. Instead, his head was lowered, as though in prayer. This pose struck Charlie as strangely unlike Billy. Never had he imagined Billy having any religious sentiments. Maybe he wasn't praying at all, just focusing his thoughts on the race. Anyway, why should it surprise him to discover that Billy was religious? Being religious didn't mean attending church or a synagogue. He was religious himself--had even been bar mitzvahed. But how often did he go to the temple? Usually only on special holidays like Yom Kippur or Rosh Hashanah, and only with his parents' prodding at that. How well did he know anyone really? He looked away from Billy and fixed his eyes again on the flag. A small breeze began to stir and ruffle its corners. Suddenly he felt goose bumps all over his arms and the inside of his thighs and the backs of his legs.

Whistles and shouts from the stands arose as the national anthem ended. The twelve riders began pulling on their helmets and fastening their chinstraps while out on the track their tuners bump-started their bikes. The engines popped and sputtered and then exploded with low throaty roars that shook the stadium bleachers.

The flagman, clad in white, gestured to the first group of six riders to move their bikes to the front line while another official lined up the bikes so their front wheels touched the chalk line. Then he directed the other six bikes to take their positions behind the front row. Since Billy had turned the seventh fastest time, he was right next to the rider who had the pole position. The top six qualifiers were given the choice of front-row starting positions in their heats. They could choose a slot tight against the infield or up high by the wall. National Number 20, the fastest qualifier, chose the inside position, so Billy was right next to him, their handlebars nearly touching.

The flagman walked over and picked up a black box that was attached to a long cord, which went directly to the light tower. This was the switch that would start the race.

The riders pulled down their visors and pushed themselves forward over their tanks. All twelve of them fixed their eyes on the light tower, waiting for the light to change from red to green. They had but one thought between them. Get in and out of the first turn at the head of the pack. On a quarter-mile track, the start was crucial. As the riders snapped their throttles open and closed, an undulating wave of thunder resonated through the stadium.

Then the light suddenly went green.

All Charlie heard was one tremendous roar, which shook the ground underneath him. It sounded as though a giant NASA rocket had been launched toward turn one. His eyes were on Billy. He watched as the rear of Billy's bike swung pendulum-like, first to the right and then back to the left, bumping handlebars with the riders next to him, and then straightening out before rocketing into turn one behind a wall of dust and nine other riders.

As the dust floated up over the stadium wall, Charlie could see four bikes, neck and neck, exploding from turn two onto the back straightaway. Billy was sandwiched in by a pack of bikes. He shot around two of them by going high into the cushion, grabbing traction, and exploding out of turn two onto the back straightaway.

The lead pack was bunched up in front of Billy as they entered turn three. He took a chance and again went high around the outside, pouring it on, sending up a high spray of sand and dust from his rear wheel. It worked. He came down tight against the infield rail, underneath three riders. He was now in fifth place. The heat race was only ten laps, so he would have to close in fast, make his move, before the top two or three riders pulled away.

The front pack of motorcycles stampeded across the start/finish line. Entering turn one, the bike directly in front of him wobbled and then the back section swung around jack-knifing. The rider tried to straighten the bike, but instead it whipped from side to side, shaking him violently like a timber wolf might shake a jackrabbit clamped between its powerful jaws. Billy locked his rear brake, and leaned hard, trying to slide underneath to avoid a collision.

As though in slow motion, the rider's body rose feet first above the seat, like he was attempting some wild handstand, while he gripped the handlebars desperately trying to stay with the twisting motorcycle. Then the front wheel folded underneath, sending the rear end of the bike high into the air and pitching the rider over the tank. The heavy mass of red, black, and white machine followed behind him, tumbling and kicking up dust, before striking the wall.

Red flags were out at once. The riders slowed their bikes as the corner men waved flags wildly. Seconds later, an ambulance came through the stadium gates onto the track. Charlie listened to the announcer as the riders coasted to the start/finish line and killed their engines. The rider who had gone down was Robby Johnson.

Charlie scrambled over to turn one. The plastic tail section of the motorcycle had been ripped completely off and lay in the middle of the track. He stepped over the guardrail onto the track's hard-packed surface. Robby lay flat on his back in the sandy cushion near the wall. His right leg was missing below the knee. Charlie looked over at his battered bike. Attached to a black metal strap above the foot peg was Robby's artificial leg. The naked flesh-colored fiberglass leg stuck straight up from the side of the bike, like it was trying to hold it down so it couldn't inflict any further damage. One of the paramedics placed an oxygen mask over Robby's mouth and nose while two others lifted his limp body slightly, sliding a stretcher underneath him.

Billy left his bike with Chuck at the line and hurried, hobbling on his hot shoe, toward the flashing red light of the ambulance. He arrived only in time to see two of the white-uniformed paramedics slide the stretcher carefully into the back of the ambulance. They slammed the doors shut and moved quickly around the front to the cab.

Billy just stood there, his helmet dangling at his side, staring at the back doors of the ambulance. Charlie saw Chuck at the line, holding Billy's bike with one hand and with the other motioning frantically to Billy to hurry.

Billy took one last look at the ambulance as it swung around on the track and sped off through the gates underneath the stadium, its siren slicing through the bright blue sky above them. He pulled his helmet back on and hurried back toward Chuck.

The officials had already begun lining the bikes up for a staggered start. Number 20, the rider in first place when the flags came out, was escorted to the front of the group. Then the officials directed the others to take their places in a staggered line up. Chuck, in the fourth place slot, was leaning against Billy's bike and working the throttle open and closed, revving the motor to keep it cleaned out.

Billy came up, threw his leg over the seat, and grabbed the throttle. Chuck pulled a rag out of his back pocket and began wiping Billy's face mask. Then he gave him a solid pat on the back and hurried off the track.

The starter motioned to the riders to see if they were ready.

Once again the engines revved to a feverish pitch as eleven riders simultaneously pulled in their clutches, clicked their engines into gear, and bent forward over the handlebars. The starter walked over to the light tower and picked up the black box while the helmeted figures kept their eyes glued on the tower.

As the light turned green, there was again this ripping explosion that sounded like it would bring the stadium tumbling to the ground. Billy's bike hurled forward, its front wheel two or three inches off the ground. He dropped the wheel down right before he began his slide into turn one, inches off the rear wheel of National Number 20. They shot out of the turn handlebar to handlebar, Billy on the outside against the wall. Halfway down the back stretch, Billy reached up and grabbed a tear-off, pulling it free, while keeping his upper body tucked down as low as he could over the tank. The clear plastic strip floated up over the heads of the riders behind him.

Charlie bit his nails while his eyes locked on Billy and National Number 20 as they thundered neck and

146

neck toward turn three. "Christ, Billy," he heard himself say out loud, "take it easy, man." Charlie knew a second-place spot would take Billy to the final, though it would be on the back line. Back line was better than no line, he thought, hoping to telepathically communicate this to Billy.

Six laps later Billy and National Number 20 were still going at it and had pulled away from the other riders. Billy had chosen to stay down tight in the groove, right off his rear wheel, but he could not grab enough traction nor come up with the additional horsepower he needed to power by and take the lead.

There were just two laps remaining, and as they entered turn three, Billy pushed his bike high into the apex of the turn. For a moment, Charlie thought that he had overshot the groove unintentionally. He watched as Billy leaned his bike hard, digging in with his hot shoe and rolling the throttle back. The bike began to lift in the center of the turn as a solid stream of white sand shot off his rear tire like water off the tail of a hydroplane. As he blasted out of turn four, his bike was in a complete power slide, crossed-up, handlebars turned all the way over against the fork lock. Down tight in the groove, National Number 20 had just exited the corner onto the straightaway. Billy torpedoed out behind him, sliding his weight back on the rear wheel. As his tire gripped the black groove of the track, his motorcycle leaped out in front by a full bike length.

Charlie watched as Chuck thrust his right fist skyward and shouted out above the thunderous tumult of the engines, "Show 'im now, Billy! Show 'im how them Ohio boys do it!"

With one lap to go, the white flag was out. Billy had dropped back down into the groove on the last lap, and when he crossed the finish line, National Number 20 was only inches off his rear tire.

Charlie was in a daze. It was unreal. His friend had just made it to the Daytona Grand National Final!

Back at the van Billy was assaulted by Chuck before he could dismount.

"What a go, Billy!" Chuck screamed, throwing his arms around Billy and hugging him before he could remove his helmet.

"Yeah, man, you really smoked 'im!" Charlie shouted, grabbing him by the arm, unable to control his emotions.

Billy slipped off his helmet. "Got a great shot into the corner on the restart," he said in short breaths. Then a cloud seemed to pass over his face. Billy pulled his leathers down around his waist. Charlie threw him one of the rags from the back of the van. He wiped the sweat from his face and neck and then tossed the rag back to Charlie. "Be back in a couple of minutes."

Charlie knew where Billy was off to. As he hurried away, Charlie suddenly recalled this vivid image of Robby's legless, prostrate body. Once the race had restarted, and he was caught up in the excitement, he had forgotten completely about the crash and about Robby. Billy must have blocked it out too. Yet not for long. Charlie was discovering new facets of Billy's character. Would he have hurried off right after qualifying for a

Grand National final to find out about a fellow rider who had been injured in his heat race?

Chuck had already removed the rear wheel and was busy with some tire irons, prying the tire free. After he pulled the tire completely off its rim, he went over to the van and grabbed a new tire. He began working its bead over the edge of the rim. This would give Billy a fresh edge for the final.

As Chuck worked on the bike, Charlie listened to the crackling voice of the announcer calling out names and positions over the roar of motors as the riders jostled and swapped places in their heats. From the pit area behind the stadium wall, he couldn't see any of the track, but he could see a thick cloud of dust rise above the infield. It floated upward and outward over the stands and into the pit, gradually thinning out, its fine particles raining down on the vans and pickup trucks, covering them with a fine white powder.

The smell of high-octane fumes and dust had apparently clogged Chuck's nose. He took out a handkerchief, blew hard into it, then opened it up, and examined the glob of black mucus inside.

"You need some help?" Charlie asked.

Chuck folded the handkerchief back up and put it in his shirt pocket. Then he returned to working on the bike. He was slipping the axle through the frame holes and rear wheel. Beneath his baseball cap, small beads of sweat had formed into a tiny rivulet that ran down the bridge of his nose and collected at its tip.

"No, I think I can blow my own damn nose, thank yuh."

"I didn't mean that kind of help," Charlie laughed, standing over Chuck.

"Grab the tire pump in the back of the van and the tire gauge out of the toolbox. The pump's behind the front seat of the cab."

Just then Billy walked up and, without saying a word, bent down next to Chuck and checked the tension on the chain.

"Well, what hospital did they take him to?" Charlie asked, setting the tire pump down in the oil-stained grass next to Chuck.

"I didn't ask," Billy said, his voice sounding as dry as the white powder that had fallen over everything. "An ambulance paramedic told me that Robby was dead when they loaded him in the ambulance."

Chuck stopped working on the bike and looked over at Billy. "You're shittin' me," he said, dropping his wrench against the rim. The sharp metallic ring of the wrench against the wheel seemed to hang in the air like an omen.

"Wish I were," Billy replied, picking up the wrench and throwing it into the toolbox. "Wish I friggin' were."

Once the plane had lifted, and the fasten seatbelt signs went off, Charlie pressed the recline button on his seat, leaned back, pulled his sunglasses out of his shirt pocket, slid them on, and closed his eyes. What a weekend! And the final! His mind had recorded every lap in detail, and now there was no room left up there for any other thoughts. It seemed he could spend the rest of his life going over and over the race and never really do it justice, or rather, do Billy justice.

Billy had had a not-so-perfect start, especially when one considers it was a front-row start. From the back row, it would have been a different story. He blasted off the start-line, rocketing into turn one, bunched up with seven to eight other guys. Miraculously, he fought his way off the corner into fourth place with twelve other bikes bunched up behind him. After three or four laps, he had moved into third, and for fifteen or sixteen laps, he tenuously managed to hold on to his spot. Then around the seventeenth lap, the line he had been taking stopped working, and the fourth-place rider closed within inches of his rear tire. Billy decided to drop down in the groove, tight against the infield rail. The three riders in front of him had decided a lap or two before that the groove was the fastest way around. The problem with remaining there was that it was nearly impossible to pass. The groove was too thin to get side by side, so all the bikes gradually ended up in a long, thin line. Slipping off the groove guaranteed dropping at least one position. Each rider perched on the rear wheel of the bike in front of him and waited for him to slide momentarily off the sticky rubbery surface onto the slippery sandy periphery.

In the early laps, Billy had burnt some of the edge off his tire, trying to power around the first two riders. The damage to his rear tire became obvious during the final laps when it began to spin without digging in. Halfway through the corner, the bike had begun to bobble as the tire lost traction. Then the next thing he knew he was sliding off the narrow black ribbon. By the end of the race, Billy had gradually dropped back to seventh. When he rode up to the back of the van, Charlie noticed that the left edge of his rear tire was shiny, bald, and threadbare.

Now Billy was off to California to give it another go.

Charlie unbuckled his seatbelt and stood up and opened the luggage compartment above his seat. He pulled a pillow out and then sat back down, placing the pillow behind his head. By now Billy and Chuck were probably somewhere on Route 10, maybe in Louisiana. They had a long drive ahead of them, and they wouldn't be back until May. Bradley had a friend in LA who owned a Harley shop. He said he could keep Chuck busy during the week and maybe give Billy enough work to pick up a few bucks. If they were careful with the money they won, it would last them until May. While on the road, they would have to stay at campgrounds, but that was part of the adventure.

Too bad there wasn't more money in racing. The purse for a seventh-place finish was pretty scanty pickings. Charlie remembered asking Chuck how much they had made. All in all, with product contingency awards and everything, it came to about $5000. And they would have to wait, maybe a month, for the companies to mail the checks.

How long would it take before Billy could make a real living at racing? He would have to be ranked in the top five riders and probably need a factory sponsorship, either from Harley-Davidson or Honda, since they were the only two companies involved in dirt track racing.

Flat-track racing wasn't a popular sport, certainly nothing like golf or tennis. Charlie doubted if the papers back home would even mention the race.

And if Billy never made it to the top five, what then? Bradley would probably sponsor him as long as he made the finals. Sponsor him and give him some piddly job at the shop to help him get through the winter. So, he would either have to make it now, in the next few years, or hang up his hot shoe. And if he decided on that, then what? Maybe back to school, night courses or a GED.

God, it all seemed like such a risky business. But risk obviously didn't bother Billy. Anyway, Billy wouldn't just throw in his hot shoe. Not Billy. He had too much pride. It would take more than a few bad seasons to discourage him, or break his spirit. No, he would stay with it as long as…long as what? As long as Pop Reymand had stayed with it? Maybe he could eventually buy Pop out, take over his shop. The thought made Charlie chuckle ironically. He pictured Billy, old, gray, and potbellied, bent over scrounging through a box of greasy parts. The comparison made Charlie feel a tinge of guilt.

And where would Praxy fit into all of this? The thing is she didn't, or wouldn't rather. But then what did he know? Maybe she would even fall deeper in love with Billy. Fall right off the cliff with him. Weirder things were possible. Yes, it was a weird world indeed. Who knew what to expect?

Like what happened to Robby.

This last thought really depressed him. He had wanted to avoid thinking about the incident. It certainly wasn't the kind of memory he wished to take back home with him. But his thoughts had somehow tricked him, and through their serpentine movements, their twistings and turnings, they had stealthily led him around to confront the grisly event. Once again he saw the bike, flat on its side, with Robby's fake leg sticking up like an exclamation point. He pushed the image from his mind.

Charlie shifted his pillow to the side and leaned his head against the cool glass while he meditated on the steady whine of the jet engines. He tried to sleep, pushing any depressing thoughts out of his mind. They rolled like clouds over the edge of the horizon until he saw before him a sky of empty blue. For a while, he floated over its vast sereneness. Gradually he felt his body being tugged downward, and then suddenly it began to spin round and round like a propeller that had become detached from a helicopter.

The next thing he knew he was lying flat on the grass, behind Chuck and Billy's van, trying to shield his eyes from the blinding spears of light stabbing him in the face. To protect himself from the penetrating glare, he raised his hand up to shield his face. He spread his fingers slowly, looking through the cracks between them, trying to discover the powerful source of light.

Then he saw it. The light was emanating from the chrome frame of a wheelchair, which had appeared from around the corner of a van. As it drew closer to him, Charlie pressed his knuckles tightly against his eyeballs, trying to rub out the white dancing ball that was threatening to etch itself permanently on his retinal walls.

Suddenly the wheelchair was pushed out of the sun into a shady pool of light near the rear of the van. It took a few seconds before he could regain his sight. When he did, he raised his head and looked up at the figure towering over him behind the wheel chair. She was a fat, dumpy girl with small narrow-set eyes and disheveled hair the color of tree bark. She shoved the wheelchair forward, right up to his face, so close that the tire almost touched it.

Charlie found himself staring at the drooping legs of a pair of gray corduroy pants. The pant legs lay flat against two bony calves. Mere corduroy and bones. Charlie's eyes traveled upwards.

Gazing down at him was this gaunt face. The eyes had wide blue circles under them. The dark, unruly hair magnified the pallor in the cheeks. Charlie looked closer. The face had a ghastly familiarity about it, yet he couldn't pin it down. There was something about the eyes and the thin line around the corners of the mouth, but there was nothing either explicit or pronounced about the face itself, other than its chalky paleness, the disheveled hair, and the blue circles.

Charlie's eyes darted to the girl, but she had already turned her face away from him, so he could see only the back of her head. Her hair looked different now! It had transformed! It was no longer straight and brown! But curly and blonde. Curly and blonde just like… just like… He shot a glance back at the guy in the chair. The pale, milky face looked down at him and grimaced. Then the ambiguous features snapped into sharp focus. It was Billy's face!

155

Charlie shuddered, banging his knee into the seat-back in front of him. Thank God! It had only been a weird dream. In a short time he'd be home. Back in school. God, what strange, bizarre thoughts. It seemed he always had the strangest dreams when he napped, never at night. He'd have to mention the vision to Praxy. Not the part about the dumpy fat girl. That was really freaky. But why not? Maybe there was something in it. Anyway, it wouldn't make sense to tell just part of it.

CHAPTER ELEVEN

Today is July the third. Tomorrow is Independence Day. What a friggin' joke. Independence Day for who? What's there to celebrate? And with who? Stockton? Yeah, he'll be a barrel of fun. This morning I asked him if I could get a TV in my room, black and white would be all right, nothing special. I'd even be satisfied with one of those cheap little jobs with a screen about the size of a toaster. Or, if not in my room, then maybe he could arrange another room for me here in the Hilton.

He gave me one of his stock answers: "Ask Phillips." Then I started laughing like a goddamn madman. I suddenly made this connection about his name. His last name was probably a sobriquet. It fit him perfectly. "Stock" and "ton." "Ton," like in "ton of." And "stock" like in "stock of." He had "tons" of pat expressions in "stock" all right, like: "I don't know." "Ask Phillips." "Take your pills." "Maybe tomorrow." His name probably helped him get the job.

During the session with Phillips earlier today, I lost it. I mentioned that I had asked Stockton for a TV. I explained to Phillips that it would help me pass the time. He told me he'd see what he could do. I told him that I didn't understand. What was there to see? I was just asking for a friggin' TV. What was the big deal? He looked at me like I was asking for tickets to a rock concert. Jesus Christ, what was wrong with a little

157

diversion? Maybe I could watch an Independence Day parade or something. The TV might even be therapeutic. Raise my drooping spirits some. Anyway, was a TV an outrageous request? Then I told him I was sick of his shit. That I was being treated like a prisoner. And that even might be acceptable if he'd level with me. Even a prisoner is entitled to know what crime he's accused of. And if I wasn't a criminal, then why was I being treated like one? What did I do? Murder somebody?

He said that there was no point in getting worked up, that getting all worked up was counterproductive. I felt like killing the baldheaded bastard. I told him to go to hell.

That really pissed him off, though he tried like hell not to show it. He stood up abruptly behind his big desk, with his chubby hands resting on its edge, and said with his fake smile that it was better to suspend for today. Then he picked up his phone and rang for Stockton to take me back to my "suite."

So I'm supposed to sit here all day and listen to this elevator music they pipe in. Or lie down in my bed and stare at the four walls. Great way to pass the day. I guess if I get super bored, I can always go over to the window and look out at the empty courtyard. Watch the grass grow. Maybe I'll get lucky and see something really exciting going on, like the old black guy riding his lawnmower around and around.

Of course, I have the notebook here. A present from Phillips. He tells me that I should write in it whenever I feel like trying to piece things together, or when I'm upset. It's a way of releasing tension. Is the notebook really for me though? Or is it a way of him knowing things about me that I don't want to tell him? A way of spying on my thoughts?

I once asked him if what I wrote in my notebook was private. Was it for me or for him? He told me that the more he knew about me, the more he might be able to help me, but if I didn't want him to read what I wrote, then he wouldn't read it. All I needed to do was write "DON'T READ THIS" on the top of the pages that I didn't want him to look at.

Sure. Simple. Sounds like a stupid idea that a junior high school teacher would come up with. Since I never trusted my teachers with my personal matters, I certainly wasn't going to trust this flake. First, he'll have to give me a reason to trust him. Until he does that, he can screw off. And that's what I told him in so many words. I said I didn't want him to read what I wrote, that I'd rather just keep it to myself. That he should think of it as therapeutic, and not to be shared, unless I expressly said so.

He agreed, for whatever that's worth.

I figured I would check him out. There's this novel we read last semester. It's called *1984*. Which is really stupid, since it's supposed to be about a future world. Anyway, there's a guy named Winston Smith. And he can't do doodley-squat without the authorities knowing about it. They're always watching him. Even when he takes a crap, though they don't say that in the story. But it's a foregone conclusion. I mean they have cameras all over the friggin' place. Winston has this special corner in his living room where he can hide. It's an alcove that's tucked out of sight in the corner where the telescreen can't see what he's doing. The telescreen is a huge screen that spies on people. You see it in all the public buildings, in the streets, plazas, restaurants, and even in the head honcho's homes. It hears and sees everything, and if you commit a crime, Big Brother, the party chief, is the first to know.

This guy Winston is so paranoid that he believes it's just a matter of time until the Thought Police get him. He's committing a thought crime by writing in his diary, and he suspects that he'll eventually be discovered.

Well, to try to see whether Big Brother is on to him, each time he writes anything in his diary, he places a particle of white dust between the last pages he has written. I think it's dust. That way, if it's gone or has shifted its place on the page, he'll know that his diary has been tampered with.

So I figured what the hell, just because it didn't work for Winston, doesn't mean it won't work me. So I thought I'd check Big Brother Phillips out.

I placed this tiny white flake of plaster, which I scraped from the wall, in my notebook, right smack in the upper right corner, close to the edge, so if he flipped through the pages, I'd know it.

He's either keeping his word or he's read *1984*. In the book, the Thought Police always made sure to replace the speck of dust when they were finished.

I must have really pissed him off today. Which is good and bad. He's not, if I had a choice, the person I would choose to sit down and spend the afternoon chatting with, but being with him is sometimes better

160

than being alone. I thought that he'd send for me later this afternoon, after he cooled off. I'm not sure talking to him really helps me much. About all his stupid sessions get me to realize is how little I know about myself. That doesn't exactly cheer me up. As he tries to help me piece together my past, I realize there are these huge blocks missing. It seems even stranger that I call it *my* past. Sometimes I feel like I'm making half of it up as I go. I mean the gaps. There are too many of them, and they are so large that I often think that I could fill them with a lifetime of experiences, but the experiences would still not put Humpty Dumpty back together again. Phillips has only helped me see the gaps. And what kind of help is that really? It's like a friggin' pest exterminator pointing out to you all the places where the termites have burrowed in the wood, and then doing nothing to rid you of them or repair the structure.

That's how I feel, burrowed full of holes. More gaps than substance. A piece of Swiss cheese. Like right now. I keep thinking about this letter. Right after I left Phillips's office, I came to my room and sat down on the edge of the bed, and then this letter thing popped into my head. Out of nowhere. Just like that. It's got to be important, surely, but why, I haven't the slightest idea. When I try to remember its contents, I'm staring at another gap. The funny thing is that when I do succeed in filling in gaps, the events that become clear and distinct seem to be isolated or disconnected from any other events. This gives them an unreal quality, as though they were invented by a storyteller who chooses to capture only certain parts of the story, and in no chronological order. So I'm just left hanging, at the storyteller's whim, his passive audience, sitting by and waiting for him to mention details that will dispel the fog.

For example, after Daytona, I can recall a few events, but they seem no clearer to me than, say, a snapshot taken at midnight without a flash. I remember that Chuck and I had started our return trip from California. I see the van, I see Chuck, I see a road, but the rest of the details have fuzziness around them. Even the races. I remember vague feelings of disappointment, and I can recall generally what happened. But only as if the events of the two months I spent out West had been told to me. If Phillips, or anyone, were to ask me about Pomona, I would say matter-of-factly that I finished fourth in my heat and third in the semifinal, and that I just missed the transfer spot to the final. But I don't really remember the friggin' race itself. And that's pretty scary. I do remember the Daytona race. I mean nearly every detail of the Daytona race is there. No big gaps at all. And the Sacramento race. I can remember more about Sacramento than I can remember about Pomona, though I'm at a loss as to why. They both were about the same time. Maybe because I nearly cashed in my chips at Sacramento.

The first word that comes to my mind to describe Sacramento is DISASTER. My Harley smoked a piston during a practice lap, which caused the rear tire to lock up as I was about to slide into turn three. I ended up plowing into a hay bale. I came to as they were bringing the stretcher over. The next thing I remember is sitting up on the stretcher and looking around for my bike,

162

while I yanked a handful of straw out of my face shield. I'm lucky to be alive. I went down at over 100 miles per hour. At the time, I remember being more pissed than shaken. We were out of the race. Just like that. So Chuck and I packed it up and then watched the race from the roof of the van. After the race, I believe we headed out for Oklahoma City.

It's funny. Right after Daytona, everything had looked so promising. I thought for sure I would make the finals in California. I remember calling Praxy, trying to sound upbeat. It was usually on the weekends. It was a way of staying in touch. I didn't have any permanent address and really wasn't much into writing. Usually on Sunday nights I'd give her a ring and tell her about the week and the race and all. That's if the race was on Saturday. If it was a Sunday race, I'd wait until Monday night. Sometimes I didn't call her at all because I'd be too busy trying to pick up some easy money at a pro race somewhere way out in the boonies. I soon found out that it wasn't so easy. This is because most of the other "hot shoes" on the circuit had the same idea. Before I knew it, it was the middle of the week, so I just told myself I'd wait until the following weekend to give her a ring.

The letter. There's something about Oklahoma and the letter. I must have written the letter about the time of the Oklahoma race. I remember writing the friggin' thing and mailing it from the post office in Tulsa. That I'm sure of. What the letter was about, now that's another thing.

For the past hour, I've been lying here on the bed, staring up at the ceiling, trying to remember the occasion for the letter. My mind closes on nothing. It's like I'm pulling on this door with everything I have and still it won't open a crack. After a while I grow tired and feel the door handle slip from my grip. My head sinks deeper into the pillow to where I can see only its white edges and the empty flatness of the ceiling. I gaze up searchingly and discover the razor-thin cracks in the plaster. For now I'm content to dwell on their simplicity. Over and over again my eyes trace their thin jagged paths along the ceiling. I feel my eyelids becoming heavy with sleep and my thoughts being absorbed by the ceiling's featureless landscape, like snowdrops descending on a frosty meadow.

Tomorrow I'll talk to Phillips. Tell him about the letter. Now I only want to rest.

CHAPTER TWELVE

"Sit down, Charlie," Praxy said softly, gesturing toward the sofa. Her eyes were red and the skin around them puffy. She dabbed at them with a tissue and then reached into her black leather purse and took out a letter that was folded over into a square. Her fingers fumbled over its edges and then slid between its folds. She opened it slowly. Her hand trembled as she passed the letter to Charlie.

"From Billy?"

"Yes." It sounded like her heart had moved up into her throat and caught there. She slumped down on the sofa beside him, resting her hand on his knee.

Charlie held the letter awkwardly in his freckled hands, as though it were some small injured bird. She watched his eyes hurry over the words.

Dear Praxy,

I don't know how to begin this letter. I find it hard to write down my ideas. They look so permanent, so final when they're written down. And sometimes they don't even look like they're mine (That can be my excuse later, if I need one). But if I don't write you now, I'm afraid I'll put it off and what I have to say won't be said or it will be too difficult later.

I was excited when I called you tonight because today was a great day for me. At least, it started out that way. Then what you had to say kind of zapped me real hard. Knocked the old wind right out of my sail, as Chuck would say. Now I'm okay, I think.

By the way, my second place finish today boosted me into tenth place in the Camel Pro points standings. And after the race, John Perkins, Honda's factory mechanic, came over to me and told me that he had heard Honda was going to sponsor another rider. He said he'd put in a word for me. Things are looking up, that is with racing.

Praxy, I don't know how to say this, but after I hung up the phone, I didn't know what to think. I felt kind of numb, and maybe a little hurt or betrayed even. And then the more I thought about it, the more foolish I felt. Why? Because I guess deep inside, I always had this feeling that things would turn to muck. They usually do. That's the story of my life when it comes to personal things. I guess what generally passes for love isn't love anyway. It's something else. Shared intimacies, maybe. Love, the kind you read about in books, or see in the movies, is about as real as the Mona Lisa's smile, but not as lasting. At least that's been my experience.

Anyway, I just wanted you to know I'm okay now. I'm sure I sounded a little shaky over the phone. Please don't worry about me. I'll be all right.

Peace,
Billy

"Seems to have taken things okay," Charlie said with a forced smile, looking up from the letter.

"You really think so?" Praxy asked, leaning back in the sofa, fixing her eyes on the vacant air. Her thoughts stuck on the word "betrayed." Regardless of how she might deny it, it seemed to fit what she was feeling inside.

166

"At least the tone of his letter seems to suggest that."

Oh, God. Things were so difficult. If feelings didn't change. But they do, she mused sadly. It's not that she loved Billy any less. She just loved him in a different way. Anyway, she was just seventeen, and seventeen was too young to make grand commitments. Billy should understand that. Love. Such a big word.

It was funny, the saying, "Absence makes the heart grow fonder." At first, she thought she'd go nuts not seeing him. He had been away since March, and now it was the end of May, but with Charlie around, she'd become less introspective and had begun to see the relationship more from a distance. Billy's absence had begun to produce the opposite effect. In the early weeks, right after he had gone, she would talk incessantly about him. Soon she became aware that it bothered Charlie. He even told her once that she had an unhealthy obsession.

It was after Charlie told her about the weird dream he had on the plane that she began to see Billy in a different light. It was this dream about her pushing around a wheelchair with this guy in it who looked like Billy. How eerie. God, what would she do with a husband in a wheelchair? Crippled for life? And there was no way on this earth Billy would quit racing, even if that's what she wanted. Also his carpe diem outlook was a bit disquieting. This idea that what matters is the here and now. Tomorrow will somehow take care of itself. Well, it doesn't exactly.

"Look, Prax, there's no point in dwelling on what we're going to say to Billy when he gets home. Or how

167

we're going to act around him. I mean, Christ, it's not like we committed a crime."

"Yeah, you're right, but I still feel bad about having told him over the phone. I should have waited until he came home. Sometimes I just think I'm a big coward."

"I kind of think that maybe Billy would have wanted it that way. He's not the kind of guy who's going to sit around and discuss it with you. Or with me, for that matter. And he's definitely not the kind of guy that would ever try to talk you out of acting on your feelings."

Feelings. No, she and Billy never really talked much about feelings. Neither about his or about hers. He would listen, but listening wasn't enough. And wasn't Billy's letter a perfect example? What did he really feel? What were the secrets of his heart? His letter had pretty much said it all, and this made her even sadder.

"Would you like a Coke or something? Think I'll have some juice," Praxy said, combing her fingers through the soft down of Charlie's hair. It was as thin and straight as the hair of a baby.

Charlie was so different from Billy. He wasn't afraid to show his feelings. When he told her about Daytona, the story and the storyteller were inseparable. He painted for her emotional landscapes that made her feel as though she had been there with him. Billy's account was like a brief summary scribbled out in crayon by the clumsy hand of a six year old. The strangest thing of all was that Billy never even mentioned this Robby guy's accident.

As she rose from the sofa, she took hold of the letter that was still in Charlie's hands, and giving it a gentle tug, slid it from his fingers.

"Sure, I'll have a Coke." Charlie closed his hands together into one fist and then bent his fingers backward, snapping his knuckles.

"Charlie, don't do that!" she said squeamishly, gritting her teeth and then punching him in the arm.

"Ouch!" Charlie laughed. "What a right. With a punch like that, you could put Tyson against the ropes." Then, unexpectedly, pogo-stick-like, he sprang out at her, grabbed her by the knees, and brought her down on the carpet.

They both laughed crazily as she struggled to twist her legs free from his grip. She rolled over onto her stomach and lifted the upper part of her body into a pushup position. Charlie let go of her legs, grabbed her tightly around the waist, and forcing his head under her armpit, rolled her over on her back again. Then, in one quick move, he slid his leg over her, caught hold of her wrists, and, straddling her, pinned her to the floor.

"Okay, Godzilla, you can let me up now. I was just tryin' to get you to stop destroyin' your knuckles. That's how you get arthritis in the joints."

"Okay, Mom!" Charlie said in small voice imitating an obedient but disgruntled child. "But only if you kiss me."

"Watch out, buster. If I'm Mom, that's incest you're talkin'," she said giddily.

"All right, den you're not my mom!" he said, this time faking a Transylvanian accident. "You're my luvely

169

victim. I just vant to zuck your blood." And with these words, his lips came down like a toilet plunger on her neck.

"Oh! Oh! Oh! Please, please do zuck my blood all you vant," she laughed. "It feels zo gute. Vut you must permit me to put zome music on first. Someting romantic, like zee Transylvanian Valtz. Or vould your prefer something vith more of a beat?"

"Vhat vould you say about putting on 'Vere Volves of London'? It's vone of my favorites."

"But first, the Coke," she said in a thick raspy voice, lifting her head from the carpet, wrapping her arms around his neck, and delivering a small peck on his lips. "Now you can get off me."

She gave him a gentle shove, and he rolled off her, backward onto the carpet on top of Billy's letter. She had dropped it when Charlie had sprung up from the sofa and tackled her.

"Charlie, you're on the letter!" The cheer had gone out of her voice.

Charlie rolled over on his side, and before he could pick up the letter, Praxy held it in her hand, staring at it. His body had bent back a corner, wrinkling and tearing one side of the letter. After attempting to smooth it out, she folded it and tucked it in the back of her jeans.

"I'm sorry. It's only a letter, you know. Unless you're going to guard it as a keepsake."

The sarcasm in his voice nailed her to the spot. "Now what's that all about? Look, Charlie, I'm just a little sensitive right now. I would think you'd understand."

"Yeah, I understand. It's not easy for me either, you know. Billy's my best friend, but piss on the letter. I'd think my feelings would be more important to you than his damn letter."

"Come on now. You have no reason in the world to be jealous," she said, cocking her head to one side and placing a hand on her hip in a gesture of mock incredulity.

"Well, Christ, Prax, what do you think? Maybe I *am* a little jealous." He walked over to the sofa and plopped down, swallowed up in its thick leather cushions. "I know it sounds crazy, but the truth is I am a little worried about what I'm going to say to him when he finally comes home."

Praxy had not moved. She watched as Charlie folded his arms, resting them in his lap. God, he was acting like a little kid.

"Afraid of what?" Her voice sounded puzzled. What was there to be afraid of? Billy understood how things were now. His letter showed that. It made her angry to see Charlie pout.

"I remember how he used to act around you, that's all. I used to think how lucky he was. And it's just that…I don't know…It's just that maybe when he's back, things might change again."

"Charlie, Charlie," she said with a mild note of frustration. She walked over to the back of the sofa and put her hands over his eyes. "What do you see now?"

"Nothing," he moped.

"Yeah, nothing. And that's exactly what you have to worry about. Nothing. Now, do you still want that Coke?" she said, drawing away from him.

"Okay," he said flatly, still brooding, his thoughts elsewhere.

"I'll be right back. And, Charlie," she said, "Billy's a big boy. He'll understand everything and we'll be friends like always. Maybe it will be a little difficult at first, for everybody, but that won't change how we feel about each other. Billy's our friend, and that won't change ever," she said with all the conviction she could muster. Then before turning to go into the kitchen, she reached around behind her and pushed the letter deeper into her jeans pocket.

CHAPTER THIRTEEN

Son-of-a bitch! He's just full of surprises. As soon as I mentioned the letter, he asked me if it had anything to do with Praxy breaking it off with me. Now, how in the hell did he know anything about that?

I had given up on him dropping by, especially after our little difference today and his suggestion that we suspend the session. But when I buzzed Stockton and told him I needed something to sleep, Phillips popped his bald head in the door and asked me if I felt like talking. I didn't say anything, so he just came in and plopped down in the chair next to my bed and asked me why I was having trouble sleeping. So I mentioned the letter. And like I said, the bastard already knew about it!

So now I know what the letter was all about. While I was gone, Charlie, my best friend, was putting the moves on Praxy. It started while I was away on the circuit. I guess I discovered too late that Charlie had no idea of the meaning of friendship. No, Charlie didn't give a shit about me. Charlie was out for number one.

Phillips wanted to know what happened when I returned from Oklahoma, how I'd handled things. I told him it wasn't all that clear. I remembered being back for about a week before I decided to see Charlie. Or Praxy. Then one night I dropped by Praxy's on my Triumph, kind of unannounced, and a little high. Charlie was there too, which didn't surprise me, though I had never set foot in her house myself. I'm sure Mr. Bishop hit it off with Charlie a hell of a lot better than he ever would have with me. Anyway, I pulled my bike next to his Honda and killed the engine. I was feeling a little fuzzy from the booze, probably because I hadn't eaten anything, and I'd chugged down several beers from the fridge.

I remembered Praxy strolling out with Charlie and meeting me by the curb. They must have heard my bike when I pulled up. She looked as pretty as ever, her thick blonde hair tied back with a fancy red ribbon. She was wearing a Billy Joel T-shirt and some faded blue Levi's.

Charlie stood there right beside her. The perfect couple, out for a moonlight stroll. Such a hip pair. Appropriately, he had on his fake aviation jacket. He offered me his hand, saying it was nice to see me, or some such crap. I didn't shake it, but instead I laughed. Then I remember taking off my jacket and throwing it at him. I told him it was his if he wanted it. That he shouldn't settle for an imitation when he could have the real thing. When I tossed the friggin' thing at him, it wrapped completely around his face and neck. I looked at Praxy. I could tell she was upset. She gave me this pathetically ironic smile and said, "Good night," and then wheeled around quickly and strutted back toward her house.

Charlie and I stood there looking at each other for the longest time, and then I finally came right out with it, broke the silence like a sledgehammer smashing through a cheap picture glass window. I asked him if he really thought that it was great to see me. To have me back. Or if that was just part of his phony, hypocritical act. I told him it just sounded so much like him. More bullshit.

I remember that it was one of those cool nights in May, and I was getting these goose bumps as large as birdshot all up and down my arms.

He tried to make me take back my jacket. I was still sitting on my bike, and he tossed it back to me and the front of it caught on the headlight. I climbed off my bike and grabbed him by the lapels, and then, grinning at him, told him I wanted him to have it, that it was a gift.

He said I was acting foolish, that he didn't want my jacket. That the damn thing wouldn't fit him anyway, even if he did want it.

I let go of his lapels and turned around and yanked the jacket off the headlight. I dropped it right there on the sidewalk in front of him and said it was his. It spread out over the gray walk like a large puddle of oil.

Suddenly I stopped talking. Phillips acted surprised. He waited patiently. A full two or three minutes must have passed. He told me I should continue. He said it was important.

But that's all I could remember. Just the jacket there on the sidewalk. Like an inky black puddle.

Phillips said it was important for me to try to remember what happened next. I made another effort, but my thoughts slipped off down this dark tunnel. He asked me about the jacket. What Charlie did with it.

I told him I wasn't sure, but I thought he picked it up and strapped it to his seat with a bungee cord.

Phillips looked confused. "Did he strap it to *his* seat or did you strap it to *your* seat?" That was really weird. I know I said he strapped it to his seat, but I really meant that I had strapped it to mine.

Then he sprang this on me. He wanted to know if Charlie looked scared. I told him I didn't know exactly. Maybe he did. I wasn't sure.

He wanted to know why I didn't know. He said that I had mentioned that Charlie and I had stood there looking at each other for the longest time. So why wouldn't I know?

Phillips wanted me to look closer. That was part of his game therapy. It just took me a few seconds to make the connection. Then I realized what he was getting at. Again I had been able to recount Charlie's actions, but not his face! Not one friggin' time had I actually, with my mind's eye, looked Charlie in the face. It's true that I had said that Charlie and I had stood looking at each other for a long time, but this was more like a sentence pulled sloppily out of my narration than it was a vivid memory. There were things I could see, and clearly, as clearly as I could see Phillip's shiny bald head. For example, the jacket. I could still recall his jacket, even the wide, floppy lapels on his jacket. And the tennis shoes he had on, but again, try as I might, I couldn't *see* Charlie's face. I could see the jacket wrapped around it, but not the face!

I broke down. I asked Philips to help me. I begged him. I told him I was at his mercy.

He put his hand on my arm, trying to calm me down. He told me he didn't know exactly what to think of the Charlie thing, but that together we could maybe sort it out. His pet expression, "sort it out." It angered me to hear him use it. It was so damn fake. So insincere. Just another of his games. Like the letter.

I tore myself free from him and shouted out that I was tired of his secrecy business, tired of being treated like some mental case. Maybe I wasn't exactly well. But for Christ's sake, would these games ever end!

I began to get nauseated, and my head felt like it was splitting down the middle. I told him that if he really didn't know anything, then maybe he should leave.

He lifted his flabby body out of the chair next to my bed. Then he stood there for a moment as though pasted to a wall. I noticed that he had on his plaid blazer with the large checkerboard patterns. Looking at him made my stomach feel like I had just swallowed a hornet's nest. If he didn't leave right away, my head would surely part in halves. He must have seen the anguish on my face. I could tell by the way he nervously repositioned his glasses on the bridge of his nose.

He turned his back to me and took two steps toward the door, and then he stopped and turned back around.

"I don't know if this will help you remember," he said with this phony Jack-in-the-Box-smile. "But I would like you to think about the name Hampton Road. Ask yourself if the name means anything." Then he opened the door and seemed to drag himself out of the room.

So, first the letter. And now Hampton Road. His second big surprise. What's next? What else will he pull out of his bag of tricks?

Hampton Road.

Sure it means something. It's right outside of town, a long stretch of road that winds through the valley. The last time I remember going out there was with…

Suddenly I have trouble breathing, like I'm drowning or something and need to scramble quickly to get up to the surface for air. Hampton Road! Another one of Phillips's secrets hurled at me like a bad dream! I roll over on my side in the bed and draw my knees into my chest. My head continues to throb and my stomach burns like I'd just gulped down a quart of battery acid. I raise a trembling hand to my forehead. It feels as cold as a corpse. I pull the cool white sheets over my shoulders and stare blankly at the wall.

CHAPTER FOURTEEN

"Nice to see you, man," Charlie said, extending his hand, his voice as tight as a spoke.

Billy was balanced precariously on his bike with his feet on the pegs and the bike keeled over on its kickstand. He stared at Charlie's outstretched hand and chuckled in disbelief. Then he leisurely slipped an arm out of his leather jacket and wiggled the rest of the jacket free from his shoulders. Balling it up as tightly as a bedroll, he threw at Charlie. He shot a glance deliberately at Praxy and then turned back to Charlie and said, "Might as well have the jacket, too."

Charlie looked at Praxy. "Good night," she said, looking at Billy and forcing a faint smile, her voice as shrill as a nail scraping against a windowpane. Then taking her eyes off him, she spun around abruptly and scrambled up the front lawn toward her house.

Charlie peeled Billy's jacket from around his neck and let it slide down his chest and land at his feet. "Christ, Billy. That was really stupid. What the hell's wrong with you anyway!" he shouted.

"You always wanted a real leather jacket, so I'm giving you mine. It's kind of a package deal."

Charlie bent over, dipping his hands in the darkness at his feet to snatch up the jacket. He tossed it back to Billy, but it caught on the headlight of the motorcycle and perched over the front fender like a giant raven.

Grinning, Billy climbed clumsily off his bike and staggered over to Charlie and grabbed him roughly by his jacket lapels. He thrust his face up to Charlie's, only inches away. The smell of sour beer was overpowering. Billy's grip tightened on Charlie's jacket until Charlie was forced to look directly into his red-tinged eyes. For a moment he thought Billy was going to rip the front right off his jacket. He panicked, not sure what to do next. Then suddenly he felt Billy relax his grip.

"I want you to take the friggin' thing. It's a gift. Really, I want you to have it. You've had your eyes on it almost as long as you've had your eyes on…on other things."

"Man, you're acting like some kind of loony. I don't want your jacket." Then trying to mollify Billy some, "Anyway, it won't fit. It's too big."

Billy whirled around awkwardly and snatched the jacket from the headlight. He held it out in front of him, inspecting it. "It just needs some care and attention, a little smoothing and saddle soap maybe. Then, just like that, before you can say 'Daytona Beach,' its old shape will vanish. It will look and feel like it was always yours," he said, dropping the jacket on the sidewalk and climbing back on his bike. "Like I said, it's yours."

He leaned over and grabbed the kick-start lever and flipped it out from the bike. Then springing into the air, he came down, delivering a solid kick. The engine sputtered and coughed and then shot tiny orange and blue flames out the rear exhaust pipes. He rolled back the throttle a couple of times to warm up the cylinders, and then let the engine die down to an idle. Its valves clacked like a dozen spoons beating out a rhythm on the bottom of a tin pan.

"Hey, look, I'm sorry about…about what happened," Charlie said, barely audibly, scooping up the jacket. "You can't expect our lives not to change, to be the same as when you left. What happened wasn't planned, Billy. It's just that Praxy and I discovered that we're…that we're…a lot alike, and because of that, we like being together. That's all."

"So, she's not your girl? Is that what you're saying? I'm just imagining things, right?" he asked flippantly.

"No, you're not just imagining things. I guess you could say she's my girl, though I don't like the sound of it. It sounds too much like she belongs to me, like I own her. Hey, look, Billy, I want you to know that I didn't mean…"

"Look, man, just forget it," Billy said dryly. "Shit just happens, as they say. Besides, I'm not in the mood or the condition to discuss it right now. Whaddayah say we take a spin? Blow this place off. The Heights gives me the creeps. There's something unreal about it."

"I don't know. Don't you think that…"

"Come on, man. She's not goin' anywhere. She'll be there when you get back. At least, I used to believe that."

"Okay, man, for old time's sake," Charlie said, trying to sound convincing. He shoved his hand into the front pocket of his jeans and pulled out his bike key. The key slipped from his fingers and fell to the pavement with a dull ring. When he bent over to pick it up, he saw a puddle of oil underneath Billy's bike, directly in front of his rear tire. As he snatched up the key and Billy's jacket, a breeze began to rustle the leaves in the maple tree overhead. A chill swept over him, raising the tiny hairs on his forearms and the back of his neck.

"Ready?" Billy asked.

"Yeah, I'm ready." Standing next to his bike, Charlie shoved the key into the ignition slot. Out of the corner of his eye, he saw a light come on. He glanced toward the house and saw a figure silhouetted against one of the windows upstairs. He twisted the key in the Honda's ignition switch, and the engine caught immediately and began humming like a low-pitched electric drill. The bike's headlight came on automatically, its beam slicing through the darkness and striking a huge oak tree.

"Come on, man, let's cruise!" Billy yelled out.

Charlie pushed Billy's jacket under a bungee cord he had strapped over the rear of his motorcycle seat and then threw his leg over the seat. "Where are we going?" he asked, snapping his knuckles.

"Hampton Road!"

Billy revved the motor three times, and then toed the shift lever down into first. The bike shot forward, the rear tire spinning a path through the oil.

Underneath the streetlamp, Charlie could make out a glimmering tire track that faded away in the thick shadows beneath the overhanging tree limbs. He pulled on his helmet and set off after Billy, following his small dim taillight.

A few minutes later they were winding down a steep hill that entered the valley. Patches of fog wafted by as they continued their descent. Charlie's face shield began to steam up on the inside, so he shoved his hand up under its lip and tried to wipe away some of the moisture. This only made things worse. The fog in the valley was heavy now, so the shield was completely vapor smeared.

Through the blur of his face shield, everything took on a ghostly impermanence. As his tires struck the uneven surface of the road, his headlight beam bounced about wildly. A few bike lengths in front of him, he could see only the watery image of Billy and his bike. It was like looking through the sides of a fish bowl. Billy's white shirt fluttered and danced in and out of focus. Only with difficulty and at intervals could Charlie see the road divider lines and the white stripe along the edge of the road.

As soon as they came to the four-way stop at the bottom of the hill, Charlie threw open his face shield. He pulled up alongside Billy and pointed to the open shield. "Hey, I can't see a thing! I'm gonna have to take my helmet off and wipe the shield."

"Just leave it open. No one's gonna hassle you about it anyway. Look at me, for Christ's sake, I don't even have a helmet."

"Okay," Charlie said, placating him.

"You worry too much."

"You're probably right."

"No, not probably," Billy grinned, wiping the condensation off his mirror with the palm of his hand. "A person who's too afraid to take a risk ends up being quite a bore. Right?"

"Yeah, sure, Billy, whatever you say," Charlie said.

"Whaddaya say we have a little fun? The jacket," Billy said, pointing to his jacket fastened down on

Charlie's seat. "You wouldn't take it as a gift, so how about winning it?"

"Winning it?"

"Yeah, it could be yours fair and square. And I'll even give you generous odds."

"I don't follow you."

"No, I'll follow you," Billy said teasingly. "It's like this. I'll let you cross the intersection here onto Hampton Road. Then I'll start counting out fifteen seconds. It's about two-and-a-half miles to Whitman Road, the first road before the stop sign at Branton. If you get there before me, and I'm giving you fifteen seconds, then you win the jacket. It should be simple. Even for you. Unless you're too afraid to have a little fun."

Charlie knew this part of Hampton Road well. He and Billy had taken night rides down it many times, winding through its twisting corners. With a fifteen-second lead, there was no way Billy could get to Hampton and Whitman before him. He had to be out of his mind. Or else it was just the booze talking.

"Okay. Why not. Fifteen seconds, right?" he said, revving his engine to clear it out.

"Fifteen seconds. Do you need more time?" Billy grinned, staring at Charlie and then hunching his shoulders, signaling to him for a reply.

"That should be more than enough." Charlie clicked the gear lever down into first and popped the clutch. The front wheel lifted about six inches as the bike bolted across the empty intersection of Burkhardt and Hampton Roads. He slammed through the gears. Second! Third! His eyes darted to the tachometer. Fourth! Fifth! Each time he slammed a gear the tack needle rose to the red line. He felt his body pushing against a wall of cool air. He turned and shot a glance over his left shoulder and then suddenly felt a wild vibration above his helmet. He had left his face shield up and the torrent of wind rushing over him had caught it, creating mad oscillations. His clutch hand flew up and slammed the face shield closed. The moisture was gone from inside it, and he felt immediate relief to be able to shut out the stinging wind.

He was about to enter the first curve. He clicked the shift lever down twice and applied the brakes, shifting his body some to the left and then leaning hard. The bike was sucked into the center of the turn, right down onto the divider line. Sweeping by at a forty-five degree angle to the road, he kept the solid white line in view up to where it disappeared into the darkness.

As he came out of the first curve, he straightened up and rolled on the throttle. The headlight's beam clawed its way through the dense air, revealing a straight stretch of road. Charlie opened the throttle all the way and tucked down level with the handlebars, his stomach flattened against the smooth metal tank. He listened to the engine winding tightly as he shifted up again into fifth gear. As he raised his head and strained his eyes to see if he could make out where the next turn began, he made the mistake of tilting his chin upwards. A violent gust of wind slipped through the crack where his shield closed against the chin guard. Instantly, the shield flew violently open, thrusting his head backwards with a jerk. He reached up blindly with his left hand and snapped the face shield down. To prevent it from flying up again, he pushed in hard on the snap until he heard it pop.

Up ahead were a series of fast snaking curves, followed by an open stretch of road with a dangerous crook in the center about a quarter of a mile before Whitman Road. This time, instead of turning and looking over his shoulder, he glanced into his handlebar mirror. No sign of Billy. He banged down a gear and applied his brakes as he approached the first curve. He had shifted down too soon. The engine revved to a breaking point, floating the valves and dropping the bike's speed suddenly. The back tire locked and pitched him forward onto the tank. The bike wobbled a little and then straightened up. His heart felt like it was about to drop out of his jacket.

As he exited the second hairpin, he quickly shifted up into third. The force of the bike's acceleration thrust him back on the seat. He leaned forward, holding on tightly to the handlebar grips. As he was about to bang the shift lever up into fourth, he heard Billy's Triumph behind him, blatting like a raging bull. Billy had just entered the hairpins! So it would be a race right to the finish! Still, with the lead he had, Billy would have to push it to the max to close up the distance.

Again Charlie looked into his mirror and this time he saw Billy's headlight come into view. God! He had zapped right through the hairpin corners! Still Whitman Road was a mile away, and his Honda could accelerate as fast as Billy's Bonneville, if not faster.

This was it then! Charlie looked down at the needle dancing wildly on the redline. Slam! Fourth! As the bike lunged forward, Charlie thought he felt the front wheel lift slightly. He leaned forward again, pitching his upper body weight over the tank. The engine sent numbing vibrations through the frame into the handlebars and into his fingertips. Slam! Fifth! He lowered his head to the level of the headlight. Using the gap between the tachometer and speedometer as a kind of gun sight, he trained his eyes on the white center divider. He straightened up slightly and shot a glance at the mirror. There was Billy's headlight, a dancing ball of light growing larger by the second.

Only one more bend in the center of an otherwise straight road, and then Whitman Road, the finish. He leaned forward again over the tank, his heart pounding madly, racing out of control. With his belly pressed against the hard metal of the tank, he had the odd sensation that he was clinging desperately to a barrel that was about to plummet over the edge of Niagara Falls.

He looked down at the speedometer vibrating under his chin. The needle was bouncing around near the 100 mph. mark. The crook in the road was right ahead. He would need to downshift, he told himself, reduce his speed to get through the turn.

He strained his eyes, searching for the bend in the center divider. There it was! He backed the throttle off and downshifted while he pressed down firmly on the rear brake pedal, shifting his weight to the right and then back to the left before straightening up. He was through the crook! He twisted the throttle open again all the way and headed down the final quarter mile of straight road toward the Whitman Road marker.

In his mirror he could see Billy's headlight shaking like a firefly trapped in a jar, spinning and fluttering about in mad gyrations. He pressed his chest to the tank as the engine began to peak. He didn't know how long he could hold it to the redline. The bike was beginning to feel like a vibrating washer with an unbalanced load. Just a few more seconds, he told himself, and it would be over.

Then he saw something amazing. Peering one last time in his mirror, he saw Billy's headlight beam suddenly disappear. One second it was there in the circle of his mirror, dead in the center, and then it was gone--had darted off like a vanishing blip on a radar screen.

Charlie came down so hard on the brakes that the back wheel locked, pitching his body forward against the tank. The screech of his back tire was interrupted by a dull explosion about as loud as a shot gun blast but much lower in pitch.

He pulled off the side of the road and released his grip on the throttle, allowing the motor to fall to a dead idle. In the hazy distance, he could make out a mixture of orange and yellow flames and black smoke rising up around the base of a tree.

Charlie flicked off the kill switch. He swung his leg over the seat and let his Honda fall over on its side in the dewy grass. His helmet slid from his hand and rolled into the gutter at the edge of the road. Fifty feet away, flattened against the side of the huge oak tree, Billy's Triumph crackled and hissed. Flames danced around it as though it were the object of some mysterious satanic rite.

A column of gray smoke rose out of the circle of flames, filling the air with the stench of burning rubber and oil.

Suddenly he thought of the black puddle under Billy's bike, and his stomach tightened convulsively as though a screw had been shoved into it and twisted off. The pain doubled him over, and for a moment he thought he was going to start retching. The fire was roaring out of control now, and he had to raise his hand to shield his face from the heat. As he did so, he instinctively stepped back, and the heel of his shoe struck against a large rock. He spun around quickly.

In the deep grass at the fringe of the circle of light lay Billy. The flames from the burning motorcycle caused the light to flicker over his body in staccato flashes, like the light from an old sixteen-millimeter movie projector. He lay stomach down against the damp earth, his neck wrenched around and his chalky face staring up blankly at the moon, his eyes wide open but vacant. A tiny trickle of blood escaped from the corner of his mouth.

Charlie stood motionless until the raging fire abated and darkness regained its footing and spread through the trees and over the damp ground.

Dazed, in a semiconscious state, he retreated to the side of the road where he had dropped his motorcycle on its side. He bent down lethargically, grabbed the handlebars, and managed to lift the bike upright. Sluggishly, he removed his jacket and dropped it in the grass at his feet. Then he slid Billy's black leather jacket free from under the bungee cord fastened to his seat and put it on.

The jacket was bigger than his own jacket, and heavier. He zipped up its front and pulled a comb out of his back pocket, running it through his hair in studied backward strokes. Suddenly he no longer felt enervated. Leaning against the seat of the motorcycle, he looked up at the ebony sky. The fog, though it lay heavy on the fields and road, had begun to part into thin cloudy wisps of grayish-white. He watched the small diaphanous clouds drift across a backdrop of faint, shimmering stars.

A tiny shiver went through him as he pulled his collar tight against his neck. The night sky made him think of New Mexico. And about him and Chuck pulling off the road and camping out under the naked stars. California was a long way from Ohio. They would need to save money. Camping was one way of doing that. He imagined crawling into his sleeping bag, looking up at the sequined night, and trying to pick out familiar constellations.

And sleep was what he longed for now more than anything else. He shoved the key into the ignition slot. Yes sleep… "Innocent sleep." How did it go? It was a line that Charlie used to show off his knowledge of the great bard. Yes, "Innocent sleep. Sleep that knits up the raveled sleeve of care, the death of each day's life." Sleep, just what he needed. But first he'd make sure everything was ready for the race tomorrow. If the bikes were tuned and prepped, he and Chuck could head out first thing in the morning.

He climbed on his bike, swung it around in the middle of the road, and sped off down Hampton Road toward town.

CHAPTER FIFTEEN

In front of Bradley's Harley-Davidson shop, he stood searching in his jacket pockets for the key to the side entrance. He pulled out some loose change and a sparkplug and fumbled around in the upper pocket of his jacket, but still no luck. Then he remembered the inner pocket, and unzipping the jacket front, he reached inside, and there they were.

He removed the keys and held them out in front of him. The light from the streetlight struck the chrome ring, sending sharp, iridescent spikes out from its edge. He studied the two keys. That was weird, he thought. He couldn't remember which key opened the side door. He tried both of them. One key wouldn't enter the key hole, and the one that did, wouldn't turn.

He pressed his face against the small window of the side door and peered inside. All the lights were off. He thought he remembered calling Chuck earlier and telling him that he'd meet him at the shop to help him dyno in the XR. Now where was Chuck?

He tried the lock once more, forcing one of the keys until it twisted off in his hand. This was ridiculous! He grabbed the doorknob and shook the door violently, causing the glass to rattle. Tomorrow they were heading out early in the morning. What in the hell was he supposed to do now?

Maybe one of the keys fit the back door lock.

He walked around to the back of the building. A circle of pale light from the small flood lamp over the garage door fell on the asphalt. He found the lock. He took the unbroken key and tried to insert it, but it wouldn't enter the lock. Then he grabbed the handle and jerked up as hard as he could. The lock catches on the side of the door banged against the holes in the door railing, but the door wouldn't budge more than an inch or so. Out of frustration, he gave it a kick, and then heard this deep bark coming from somewhere behind him.

He spun around just in time to see a huge German Shepherd spring onto the chain-link fence that separated Bradley's property from the house behind the garage. Its head was as huge as a bear's and the hair on the nape of its thick neck stood up like quills on a porcupine. It repeatedly threw itself against the fence, growling and snapping wildly, its huge canines opening and closing on the wire mesh.

Charlie bent over and began searching recklessly through a pile of scrap metal to the right of the garage door. If he could only find a metal bar or something to force the side door a little, right between the lock and the doorjamb, then maybe the door would pop open and he could get inside.

As he dug though the pile, the dog's howling continued. He tore a brick loose from under a pile of scrap wood and hurled it at the fence. It only made things worse. The dog went crazy, snarling and yelping and biting at the fence. Charlie saw a light go on in the house. Sweat began to collect on his brow. He wiped his forehead with the sleeve of his leather jacket. Turning back to the pile, he shoved an old wooden pallet to the side. Behind it was a metal rod about an inch in diameter. He pulled it from the pile. Holding it up to the floodlight above the garage door, he could see that it was a kickstand.

Quickly he slid back around the corner to the side door. He could feel the blood throbbing in his temples, as sweat dripped down his forehead. Forcing the flat end of the kickstand between the edge of the door and the doorframe, he pushed with the weight of his entire body. The bar slipped out of the groove and fell clanging to the concrete pad at the base of the door. As he stooped to retrieve it, he was caught in the swath of a bright white light coming from the headlights of a car that had just swung into the driveway.

Christ, it was about time, he thought. He was beginning to think Chuck had forgotten all about Daytona. While he raised his hands to his eyes to shield them from the glare of the headlights, he heard two car doors slam.

"Please move away from the building and raise your hands above your head!"

What! He let the kickstand fall to the ground and then held his hands over his head. What a night this was turning out to be. Now he'd have to waste time explaining all the key business to the police. Well, all they'd have to do is call Bradley, and he'd straighten everything out.

He squinted into the sharp light, trying to make out the features of two dark figures.

"Don't move!" one of the men shouted, taking a few steps toward him.

As the taller of the two figures moved closer, he could see his face clearly. He was a middle-aged policeman, maybe around thirty-eight or forty. His upper lip was completely covered by a neatly trimmed black mustache clipped squarely at its ends, and his small, dark eyes, set wide apart, looked tense and alert. Although he hadn't drawn his gun from the holster at his side, the top of it was unfastened and his right hand was resting lightly on the gun's shiny chrome handle.

"What's your business here?"

"You see, officer, I was supposed to meet Chuck Jarvis. He's my tuner. We're gonna head out tomorrow for..."

"So what's with the bar?" he said, gesturing toward the kickstand that lay on the ground near Charlie's feet.

"Well, the darn key broke off in the door, so I thought maybe I could force the door some and..."

"The motorcycle checks out," the other policeman said as he came up beside the officer questioning Charlie.

"Where you comin' from?" the one with the mustache asked.

"My girlfriend's house. I mean from a friend's house. She's not really my girlfriend now."

"Where's this?"

"Up in the Heights." He wondered what this had to do with anything.

"And your name?"

"Billy Solinski."

"You have some identification on you?" the other officer asked. His voice was softer. He was older than the mustached policeman, old enough to start thinking about retiring. He looked like the kind of guy who should be taking his grandson night fishing instead of cruising around in a patrol car.

"Sure, officer." He always kept his wallet in the inner pocket of his leather jacket, whenever he went for a ride on his motorcycle. That way there was no chance of it falling out of his back pocket. He reached into the inside of his jacket. "That's funny. I must have left it at home," he said, withdrawing his hand.

"There was a motorcycle accident down in the valley, on Hampton Road. Apparently there were two motorcycles involved. A witness identified a motorcycle with a plate number beginning with DM6, the same as your plate. That is your Honda parked in front of the building, isn't it?"

He felt short of breath all of a sudden, like he had swum a lap under water. He inhaled deeply. The air felt heavy in his lungs, as heavy as the thoughts inside his tired brain, thoughts that began to flail around wildly trying to keep above the surface of a wave of unrecognizable fear that threatened to swallow him. He felt his face grow pale and bloodless and his knees weaken.

"You okay?" the older policeman asked, grabbing him gently by the arm and steadying him.

"Yeah, I think so. I don't know what came over me." He was perspiring profusely. Silver beads of sweat stood glistening on his forehead like tiny rhinestones.

195

"Is that your Honda out front?" the mustached officer asked again.

"My Triumph, you mean?"

Surprised, the officers looked at each other. "Why don't you step around to the front of the shop with us?" said the taller officer. His voice had become suddenly stiff and authoritative.

"Sure." He felt the old guy's hand holding on to his arm to catch him if he stumbled.

The younger officer, the one asking all the questions now, unclipped a flashlight from his belt and flicked it on, pointing the beam at the tank of the motorcycle. "Says Honda right there."

What the hell was going on? He swallowed hard and his throat felt dry. That wasn't his bike. It was Charlie's bike. But then why was Charlie's bike parked in front of the shop? His eyes darted around in the dark, searching. Where was his Bonneville! Maybe he had borrowed Charlie's bike! But then, wouldn't he have remembered borrowing it? Nothing seemed to make any sense. Or maybe it did. Was this one of Chuck's silly pranks? Chuck could be a real practical joker. Maybe he and Charlie were just clowning around, trying to rattle him, get him worked up, so they could get a good laugh out of it all. That was it. While he was out back, they had swapped his bike for Charlie's.

But the police?

They didn't look like they were part of someone's practical joke.

"I think you better come along with us. We can straighten all of this out down at the station." The tall, mustached officer reached for a pair of handcuffs dangling from his belt.

"Let me handle this, Pete," the old policeman said softly, laying his hand gently on Charlie's arm. "Everything's gonna be all right, son. Whaddaya say you come along with us, and we'll give your parents a call?"

"Yeah, sure."

"Where do you live anyway?" asked the old guy, while his partner stepped brusquely over to the cruiser and jerked open the front door.

"Brown Street."

"What's the address?" asked the one called Pete, reaching into the cab of the car for a notepad he had on the dash.

Then he panicked. His address. He couldn't remember it. No fixed number came to mind. He had no problem remembering the name of the street, Brown Street, but the number. What was the number? He wasn't even sure how many digits it had, though he believed there were three.

What was happening to him?

"I…I'm not sure," he uttered dumbfounded.

"What do you mean you're not sure!" shouted Pete, visibly angry now, as he withdrew his head from the cab.

"I…I…don't know. I just can't…"

"What's your phone number then?" he fired off.

"My phone number? It's 745-3607."

"Good, son. We'll give your folks a call as soon as we get down to the station." He let himself be led toward the cruiser by the old man's slow, measured steps.

197

Charlie listened to the gravel crunch under his feet, though he felt no tangible connection with it. His own feet seemed to strike the ground without any force or weight as though the ground underneath him retreated each time the soles of his shoes attempted to establish contact.

As they neared the cruiser, he heard an occasional hiss and pop coming from the car's engine as it cooled down and shrank. Other than the sound of the gravel and the hiss and pop of the engine, everything around him seemed deathly quiet. Time itself had stopped, and the world had become suddenly motionless, strangely inert. Only he and the old man seemed capable of any movement. They glided arm in arm toward the back of the car, their steps as light as unmapped tomorrows.

CHAPTER SIXTEEN

Praxy sat in one of the hard plastic chairs in Dr. Phillips's office. She had an old issue of *Newsweek* on her lap and was flipping mechanically through the pages. She looked up from the photos to the dull green walls of his office and felt her stomach harden. Charlie's mother had called her and explained that Charlie was showing signs of recovery and that Dr. Phillips thought it might help Charlie to have Praxy visit him.

Since the night of Billy's death, she had not seen Charlie. She had called Mrs. Parker only once, and when she'd asked about Charlie, Mrs. Parker had said only a few words and then had begun sobbing hysterically. Praxy had tried to console her, and when she'd hung up the phone, she too had begun to cry. No one really knew what was going on. There were only these terrible rumors about a nervous breakdown.

When Mrs. Parker called her on the phone yesterday, she told her that Charlie had some kind of amnesia. She said the doctor was trying to get him to remember. Right now he didn't recognize her. And he kept insisting that he was Billy Solinski.

Mrs. Parker told Praxy that Dr. Phillips worked for the courts and that Charlie needed to remain in his custody. The authorities mentioned that it was in Charlie's best interest, so Mrs. Parker and her husband readily agreed. When Mrs. Parker had tried to visit him once, he had gotten angry, contending that she was Charlie Randolf Parker's mother, that they were all nuts or playing some sadistic game with him, and then he had withdrawn, not saying a word to anyone, not even to Dr. Phillips.

Finally the doctor had rung for an orderly to escort him to his room. This was unbearable. She and her husband didn't know what to do. They had never been faced with anything like this. They also had been told that the police needed to investigate the circumstances of Billy's death in greater detail. There were a number of questions that had to be answered, and only Charlie could answer them. Yet he couldn't cooperate until his present condition improved.

When Mrs. Parker called Praxy on the phone, she sounded fine at first. She said Dr. Phillips had telephoned her and informed her that Charlie's memory appeared to be improving some, but there were certain matters that Charlie needed to confront before more progress could be made. Then she broke down sobbing. Praxy remembered squeezing the receiver in her hand and then holding it away from her. She tried desperately to think of something to say, something that would ease the hurt. But words would not come, so she stood leaning numbly against the cold tiles of the kitchen wall, waiting for Mrs. Parker's wave of relentless tears to ebb.

When Praxy heard the door open, she closed the magazine and set it on the table next to her. A short, fat man with a bald head and thick glasses stood over her.

"Hi, I'm Dr. Phillips," he said, extending his hand warmly and greeting her with a professional smile.

Praxy rose and shook his plump little hand. "Hi, I'm Praxy Bishop." His hand felt incredibly small and soft for a man. His tiny brown eyes stared out at her from behind thick lenses. Feeling uneasy, she averted her eyes from his and stared instead at his gray and white striped tie. She noticed a coffee stain etched into its silky fabric.

"I'm glad you could come. I assume Mrs. Parker told you that Charlie's condition has improved some," he said, gesturing for her to sit down and then turning abruptly and shambling over to his desk.

The seat of her jeans had become sticky from sitting on the hard plastic chair. With her left hand, she reached around behind her and gave the clinging denim a small tug before grabbing the sides of the chair and easing herself back down in it. "Mrs. Parker said that you thought I might be able to help." Then, clearing her throat, she said, "Doctor, does Charlie really believe he's someone else, that he's Billy Solinski?"

"Often a traumatic experience, such as Charlie had, will be followed by withdrawal. Sometimes the withdrawal is brief, and sometimes it lasts for months, or even years. It depends on how painful it is to face the thing that is being repressed. Well, Charlie has definitely repressed a large range of memories that, if confronted, would create great pain. His solution has been to shift relations in his world where he has become Billy. This serves at least two purposes. One, through denial, Billy remains alive, if not so well. And, two, Charlie is punished. In his own mind Charlie has become repugnant, though he can't seem to understand exactly why. His ultimate goal is to erase him completely."

"I don't understand. What do you mean when you say Charlie is punished? Or that Charlie, pretending to be Billy, wants to punish Charlie? For what?"

He leaned back in his leather chair and crossed his arms over his huge stomach. "Because he feels Charlie is responsible for Billy's death."

"But that's crazy! Charlie and Billy were friends. Charlie thought that Billy was...was a sort of hero. He would never in a million years think of hurting Billy. I know!"

"Praxy, just because he feels somehow responsible for Billy's death, doesn't mean that he is. But then there are other things, police matters that need to be looked into and set straight."

"Police matters? I don't understand," she said with a look of puzzlement. "Surely you don't believe that Charlie had anything to do with Billy's death!"

"Why, no," he said, not altogether convincingly. "But Charlie does believe he's responsible. That's what's important. And that's why I asked Mrs. Parker to call you. His first step to recovery will be realizing who he is. I think you can help him do that."

"How? I'll do anything to help him, but...but...I'm not sure how I'm going to handle this. I mean, should I call him by his name? Should I just go along with him? Pretend that he's Billy?"

"I don't know. You'll have to see how he reacts. Your presence alone might be enough to bring him out of his withdrawal. He's close to realizing the truth. I've taken him that far. Will you try?"

"Okay," she said, her voice barely audible. Sure she would try. But it wouldn't be easy for her. Every single day for more than a month now, she had relived that night. Billy sitting there on his motorcycle in the dark, looking at her as though she had betrayed him. And then his last words to Charlie. "Might as well have the jacket too." How many times she had felt those words stabbing at her heart. Over and over again, she had tried to imagine what she might have said to Billy, how she might have at least attempted to explain…how people change, how she still loved him, and wanted to remain loving him, but not like before. She could have said so many things that night to reach him, to pull him back, to show him that she still cared as much as ever, but instead she had turned from him, and left him to himself. And why? Because of her silly pride.

"Do you think I'll really be able to help him, Dr. Phillips?"

Phillips pushed his chair back from the desk and then stood behind it staring down at its slick top as though he were searching for something to say. "I don't know," he finally said, pushing his glasses back onto the bridge of his nose. "I'm just hoping your presence can somehow help him remember who Charlie is. Right now, that's all we can hope for." He opened his desk drawer and placed the pen he had been doodling with inside. Then he stood up, lumbered around from behind his desk, and headed toward the door, his steps heavy and measured. Turning to her, he cleared his throat and said, "I'll send him in." The door clicked shut behind him.

She started when she heard the door close. Alone now, she tried to focus her thoughts on something mundane to escape the dread she was now feeling when she thought of facing Charlie. She again picked up the magazine from the end table, flipped through the pages, and then quickly set it down. This office gave her the creeps. She felt out of place. She felt like a prisoner among its cheap institutional starkness and tawdry furnishings: the plastic chairs; the metal end table covered with scratches and back issues of *Time* and *Newsweek*; the bulky maple desk that swallowed up most of the office space; the dingy metal filing cabinet with gray paint flecking off; and the brown tile floor, scuff marked with black indelible lines where furniture had been dragged carelessly over its thinly worn surface. There was no personal touch to the place at all. Nothing matched. It was as though all the objects of the room had been forced, against their wills, to share the same prison. Even the afternoon light, seeping through the faded green drapes, didn't belong, but had made a wrong turn at the window and was now forced to keep company with the drab objects inside.

Feeling asphyxiated by the cramped space of the small office, Praxy felt the sudden need to get up from the chair, to move around a little, and get her lungs pumping. She walked over to the window and pushed the flimsy green drapes farther apart to let in some more light.

Behind her, she heard the door open.

"Hi, Prax."

She froze. The voice was Charlie's, but changed. It was a bit lower and had a strained quality about it. Her knees felt suddenly flimsy. She turned slowly around from the window. Feeling the need to steady herself, she rested the palm of her hand on the back of Phillip's chair.

Immediately she noticed how thin his face had become and the dark shadows under his eyes. "It's good to see you," she said feebly.

"This is a real surprise. Phillips didn't tell me you were coming by, not until just now." Charlie smiled, a tense thin-lipped smile.

"I miss you," she said. "I've been worried about you. So has your mother. I talked to her yesterday."

"My mother," he said with a sickly laugh. "How would she know anything about me? She's avoiding me like the plague." Then more seriously, "I haven't seen her once since I've been here. So, how's everything with you?" he said, stroking his hair back lightly with his fingers.

"Okay, I guess." Suddenly her breath caught in her throat. The ducktails! Charlie never wore his hair in ducktails. Nervously she began to rotate her class ring, twirling its wide gold band around her finger.

Charlie looked down at her soft white hands and at the sparkling ring. Her hands were so small and fragile. All at once, she stopped fumbling with the ring and dropped her hands to her sides.

"Charlie's ring?"

"Yeah. I haven't taken it off, not even when I bathe, not since…that night."

"What night?"

"The last night I saw you," she said, wondering now if she had rushed things. "You know, I had a really weird feeling. I didn't want you to go with him. I sat down at the kitchen table, waiting for you to come to the back door. I was fuming about what he had said to me. I remember turning the ring over and over again on my finger, looking at it under the kitchen light. And then later, when I went upstairs, I heard the both of you drive off."

"You didn't want me to go off with him? What are you talkin' about?"

"I could tell he was hurt, or else he wouldn't have said what he did."

"He wouldn't have said what he did?"

"You know, about you taking his jacket, how you might as well have it too. He made it sound like you had taken something from him that didn't belong to you. You can imagine how that made me feel."

Praxy thought she saw a faint glow of recognition in Charlie's tense blue eyes as he stood motionless in the middle of the room. A few moments passed, and then he turned and plopped down in the chair where Praxy had been sitting, burying his face in his hands, his long fingers spreading over it like prison bars. When he finally looked up, the light from the window above played on his pale face, revealing the hard lines of his nose and forehead and the sunken contours of his cheeks. His haggard appearance suggested a man in his late twenties, not a boy of eighteen.

206

Looking down at him, his shoulders slumped down in the chair, she thought she might burst into tears.

Then, suddenly, with a kind of forced animation, he lifted his face up to hers, with this ghastly, pathetic smile spread over it. "Phillips says I'll be out of here soon! That'll be great! I bet that old Bradley's wonderin' when the friggin' hell I'm gonna turn up."

She took a step backwards. His eyes looked desperate and pain swollen, and his mouth, the way he forced his lips to curl up at the end, looked more like the snarl of a scared dog, than a smile. Though he frightened her, there was a part of her that wanted to grab him up in her arms and cuddle his head against her breasts, and tell him that it was all a terrible nightmare, that when he woke up, things would be normal again.

"Look, I want you to know something," she said falteringly, and then moving toward him, she reached down and gently touched his arm.

He sprang out of the chair, almost turning it over. "I've already missed a couple of important races, you know!" And then with great excitement, he began nervously pacing back and forth, not once turning to look at her. "I can't afford to do that, you know. I didn't quit friggin' high school to spend my time sittin' around here!" He stopped pacing and stood facing the window, his back toward her. The room grew morbidly silent. After a full minute, he spoke. "Praxy, you think you can do me a small favor?" He waited.

"Sure." Her voice wavered.

"Call Bradley and tell him not to worry. Tell him Phillips says it will be no time before I'm out of here."

"Okay." She shut her eyes, pressing down tightly on her eyelids with her forefinger and thumb, trying to hold the tears back. "You take care now," she said. "It was nice seeing you."

She waited for him to turn around and say good-bye, but he just stood there with his back to her as though he were counting the minutes until she would be gone. Slowly, she reached for the doorknob, placing her hand on its cold metallic surface. She twisted her body around and took one last look at him and then quietly pulled the door open. Phillips was standing in the hall outside.

"And, Prax," Charlie said softly, his voice like some lone wanderer lost in a vast wilderness of numbing regret, "if you see Charlie," he moved away from the window, the afternoon light against his back, "tell him…just tell him, I'm okay."

"Why don't you tell him, Billy?"

"What!" Charlie spun around, squinting into the light, his eyes on Phillips's chair. "Charlie, what are you doing here?" he shouted. His hand rose, trying to block out the light streaming in from the window behind the desk.

Praxy stared at Phillips. He had heard Charlie's scream and now stood right outside the door. He gestured to her to go back in. Then he pulled the door closed, leaving a small opening.

"Why didn't you tell me Charlie came here with you?" he said, turning back around to Praxy.

"Why…why, I thought that you knew," she said, unable to keep her voice from trembling.

"I thought I needed to see you too. You see, Billy, there's something I have been meaning to tell you, but just couldn't."

"Meaning to tell me?"

"Yes, about Hampton Road. About our last ride together."

"Our last ride together? Hampton Road? Look, Charlie, I don't know why you're here, and I don't even care. You have what you want now. Things have worked out all right for you. I just need some time for things to work out for me. And I don't think I need your help."

"I think you do. Don't you understand? Well, you will. You'll see I'm the only one who can help you. I'm like some sudden wind of truth that just blew in through the crack under the door. Kind of uninvited, you see. But necessary to tear to pieces the lie you're living. Remember that poem Mrs. Graystone read to us? I'm the wind in that poem."

"what if a much of a which of a wind
gives the truth to summer's lie;
bloodies with dizzying leaves the sun
and yanks immortal stars awry?"

"Okay, Charlie, you know, you always thought you were so clever with words. Why don't you just slip back out the door and take all your cute little words with you? Save them for Praxy. I'm sure she appreciates them."

"Look at me. Look at me real close. Look at my face. What do you see?"

"The friggin' light!" he shouted, averting his eyes from the chair. "You're right in the light! I can't see anything clearly. You're always in the light!"

"Let me help you. About that night. I want to talk about the accident. You see, I don't know why I didn't tell you."

"I don't know what you're talking about!"

209

"Look at me. You haven't been able to see me since that night. Do you know why? Because you're living in a dream world, and your phony little universe is about to break in two."

"what if a dawn of a doom of a dream

bites this universe in two,

peels forever out of the grave

and sprinkles nowhere with me and you."

"It's time to step into the dawn and out of your dream, out of the phony lie you've been living."

"You're the one who's nuts! I don't know what in the hell you're up to, what you're tryin' to prove, but I know that I don't have to stay here and listen to…"

"Yes you do. You've known all along. The fireball, Billy. Remember the fireball? You want to see me? You want to see behind that fiery mask that you put on me? Then you must see the fireball for what it really is, the fireball that burst over the field on Hampton Road the night you died, Billy. Yes, Billy, you died that night!"

"You're out of your friggin' mind!"

"Yes, that's right. I am out of my friggin' mind. But you know something? So are you. You have been for some time. And you know why you can't see me? Because you don't want to. Because if you did…"

"Get out of here, goddamn it! Or I'll…I'll…I'll make you wish you had!" Charlie stepped closer to Phillips's swivel chair and then thrust his hands up in front of his face, as though to block out the light streaming through the space between the drapes. His face was full of pain and disbelief.

"What's wrong? Having trouble seeing again? It's not the sun that's in your eyes. It's the truth. And the truth is you don't

exist. Billy doesn't exist. He died that night on Hampton Road! Don't you remember? You were there. Come on. I'll try to help you. Remember the night? It was cool, cool and...

"Foggy."

"Yes, that's right. Now you remember. It was cool and foggy."

"And there was some kind of bet."

"Great! What was the bet about? Think now!"

"It had to do with a race."

"And the jacket? How about the jacket?"

"Yes, a jacket. I remember a jacket. There was something about earning a jacket."

"Whose jacket was it?"

"It was...I don't know. I can't remember."

"Let me help you remember. Let's go back. There was something before the race. Something that you should have said, but you kept quiet."

"I don't know what you're talking about! It was a fair race! Anyway, it wasn't my idea!"

*"That's right. It wasn't **your** idea."*

"He's the one who wanted the race, not me!" Charlie was screaming now. "I didn't want his jacket! There was nothing of his I wanted! But he didn't see it that way! He felt like I had cheated him, that I had taken advantage of him. Of our friendship. And he wanted to get even!"

"But this time you had an ace in the hole, right? This time he wouldn't win. Because you knew something and you weren't telling."

"It's not true! You're a liar!"

"If I'm a liar, you know what that makes you, don't you?"

"But I didn't know!"

"You know what that makes you then?"

"Goddamn it! I didn't know that Billy would…would…"

"But in front of Praxy's house, you saw it, and you kept quiet. You saw the path of oil under the streetlight. Then again, at the stop at the bottom of the hill, under his bike, on his back tire, you had another chance to say something. Didn't you? Didn't you!"

"Yes, for Christ's sake! I saw it! But I didn't really think…no I didn't really think that…that it mattered. I mean, a little oil. What was a little oil?"

"Charlie, you were his best friend. Why didn't you tell him?"

"I don't know. I mean it's not like I really thought that…"

"Was it Praxy? Were you afraid of losing Praxy, Charlie? Was that it? Were you really that insecure? Billy was your friend, Charlie. You were at Daytona together. It was at Daytona that you saw what kind of person Billy really was. You saw what was important to Billy, Charlie. It wasn't just his racing. No, Billy didn't think only of himself. He wasn't like you, Charlie. When Billy won his heat race, remember how excited you and Chuck were? Billy was excited too. He had transferred to the final of his first Grand National race. But that wasn't what occupied his thoughts right after the race. No, Charlie, he wasn't thinking about himself only. He was more concerned about Robby Johnson, more concerned about Robby Johnson than he was about his future. Was Billy really someone you had to worry about, Charlie?"

"What do you want from me?" he said desperately. "I told you I didn't think about the oil! I saw it! Sure I saw it! And maybe somewhere, way in the back of my mind, tucked away in some little corner, I made a connection with the oil and the possibility that…that Billy might crash. But I didn't really want that to happen. Don't you believe me? I didn't want Billy to get hurt."

"Bye, Charlie. I have to go now."

"Wait! Don't go! Please, don't go! Tell me you believe me. I need to hear it from someone."

"But I must go. You see, Charlie, you're on your own now. And you're the only one who can help you. You must believe what you want me to believe. Don't you get it? When that happens, you can let Billy sleep. You can sprinkle nowhere with me and you. Bye, Charlie."

"Wait! Come back!"

"It's time I leave, Charlie. It's time I leave and take Billy with me, don't you think so?"

"Wait! Don't go yet! Please, don't go yet!" Charlie screamed, clambering over the desk and lunging at the vacant air. As he toppled over the desk, he struck the empty chair, sending it crashing over on its side.

Phillips was in the room now, and he had Praxy by the arm. "He's going to be all right. Just leave him there, and I'll get some help. It's all on tape, right in my desk drawer. There's enough there to convince anyone he isn't in any way culpable."

"So that's it! Your job hasn't been to help him but to see if he had anything to do with Billy's death!" she screamed out, tearing free from his grip.

"No, that's not it. Don't you see? He's made a gigantic breakthrough."

"Guilty until proven innocent! Is that how it is Herr Doctor? Well, in that case, I'm glad I could be of some use to you," she said bitterly as she rushed behind the desk to where Charlie had fallen.

For a few moments, he just lay there motionless, stretched out on the floor, one hand around the leg of the overturned chair. Then, like a hapless spider brought too close to the flame of a candle, he slowly, mechanically drew his legs in against his chest and curled his slender body into a ball. Praxy listened to his muffled sobs as he squeezed his freckled hands into tight fists.

She sat down next to him on the cool tile floor. Evening had come on quickly. The thick shaft of light from the window above them traversed the length of the dusk-filled office. In its pale beam, minuscule particles of dust floated about randomly, colliding with each other like asteroids hurled out of their orbits into the chaos of indifferent space. She put her arms around Charlie and pulled him into her, gently smoothing back his ducktails. How he must have loved Billy, she thought, more than Phillips would ever know. It didn't seem fair that Billy was dead. It wasn't fair to Billy, to Charlie, or to her. But then how fair was life? Maybe the problem was that people expected too much out of life. They expected life to be fair, but they didn't understand. What did oily tires know about fairness?

She placed her slender hand over Charlie's fist and tenderly put her fingers under the tips of his fingers, slowly prying open his hand so she could slip her own hand inside his. In this crazy universe, there is only one truth, she suddenly realized, only one truth that can save us. Charlie had loved Billy, and since Billy's death, he had, out of fear, ceased to love anyone, especially himself. Love was the truth he needed to rediscover. And until he could love himself, he would shut the rest of the world out forever.

ABOUT THE AUTHOR

Most of his adult life, Michael has lived overseas (Peru, Morocco, Israel, and Taiwan), teaching high school literature and technology. Michael and his family currently live in Lima, Peru. Apart from writing fiction, Michael has published numerous academic articles about literature and writing, and in 1985, Gwendolyn Brooks, poet laureate of Illinois, presented him with *Virginia English Bulletin's* first place writing award.

Novels:

Hampton Road (2004)

In Deep (2011)

Cupiditas (2012)

Evil's Root (2012) – a compilation of *In Deep* and *Cupiditas*

EMMA: Emergent Movement of Militant Anarchists (2013)

Our Darker Angel (2013)

The Bed Sheet Serial Killer (2014)

A Lethal Partnership (2014)

Sanctimonious Serial Killers (2014) – a compilation of *The Bed Sheet Serial Killer* and *A Lethal Partnership*

Made in the USA
Coppell, TX
05 April 2020